Acting Edition

Poor Yella Rednecks

Vietgone Part 2

by Qui Nguyen

Original Music by
Shane Rettig

FOR PRODUCTION INQUIRIES

UNITED STATES AND CANADA
info@concordtheatricals.com
1-866-979-0447

UNITED KINGDOM AND EUROPE
licensing@concordtheatricals.co.uk
020-7054-7298

Each title is subject to availability from Concord Theatricals Corp., depending upon country of performance. Please be aware that *POOR YELLA REDNECKS* may not be licensed by Concord Theatricals Corp. in your territory. Professional and amateur producers should contact the nearest Concord Theatricals Corp. office or licensing partner to verify availability.

No one shall make any changes in this title(s) for the purpose of production. No part of this book may be reproduced, stored in a retrieval system, scanned, uploaded, or transmitted in any form, by any means, now known or yet to be invented, including mechanical, electronic, digital, photocopying, recording, videotaping, or otherwise, without the prior written permission of the publisher. No one shall share this title(s), or any part of this title(s), through any social media or file hosting websites.

For all inquiries regarding motion picture, television, online/digital and other media rights, please contact Concord Theatricals Corp.

MUSIC AND THIRD-PARTY MATERIALS USE NOTE

Licensees are solely responsible for obtaining formal written permission from copyright owners to use copyrighted music and/or other copyrighted third-party materials (e.g. artworks, logos) in the performance of this play and are strongly cautioned to do so. If no such permission is obtained by the licensee, then the licensee must use only original music and materials that the licensee owns and controls. Licensees are solely responsible and liable for clearances of all third-party copyrighted materials, including without limitation music, and shall indemnify the copyright owners of the play(s) and their licensing agent, Concord Theatricals Corp., against any costs, expenses, losses and liabilities arising from the use of such copyrighted third-party materials by licensees. For music, please contact the appropriate music licensing authority in your territory for the rights to any incidental music.

IMPORTANT BILLING AND CREDIT REQUIREMENTS

If you have obtained performance rights to this title, please refer to your licensing agreement for important billing and credit requirements.

POOR YELLA REDNECKS was originally commissioned and developed by South Coast Repertory and Manhattan Theatre Club. The play received a world premiere co-production by South Coast Repertory (David Ivers, Artistic Director; Paula Tomei, Managing Director) on March 30, 2019. The performance was directed by May Adrales, with scenic design by Arnulfo Maldonado, costume design by Valérie Thérèse Bart, lighting design by Lap Chi Chu, original music/sound design by Shane Rettig with arrangements by Kenny Seymour, puppet design/direction by Sean Cawalti, and projection design by Jared Mezzocchi. The Stage Manager was Kathryn Davies, and the Dramaturg was Kimberly Colburn. The cast was as follows:

TONG . . . . Maureen Sebastian

HUONG/THU/SAN/COP . . . . Samantha Quan

QUANG/CHRIS . . . . Tim Chiou

NHAN/LITTLE MAN/BOYFRIEND/
COWBOY/2ND GROCER . . . . Eugene Young

PLAYWRIGHT/STAN LEE/IMMIGRATION OFFICER/
BRITISH NARRATOR/BOBBY/
TOMMY/GROCERY BOY . . . . Paco Tolson

POOR YELLA REDNECKS received a world premiere co-production by Manhattan Theatre Club (Lynne Meadow, Artistic Director; Chris Jennings, Executive Director) at Manhattan Theatre Club's Stage I Theatre on November 1, 2023. The performance was directed by May Adrales, with scenic design by Tim Mackabee, costume design by Valérie Thérèse Bart, lighting design by Lap Chi Chu, original music/sound design by Shane Rettig with arrangements by Kenny Seymour, design by David Valentine, puppet direction by Jon Hoche, dance choreography by William Carlos Angulo, and projection design by Jared Mezzocchi. The Stage Manager was Alyssa K. Howard. The cast was as follows:

TONG . . . . Maureen Sebastian

HUONG/THU/SAN/COP . . . . Samantha Quan

QUANG/CHRIS . . . . Ben Levin

NHAN/BOYFRIEND/COWBOY/2ND GROCER . . . . Jon Hoche

PLAYWRIGHT/LITTLE MAN . . . . Jon Norman Schneider

IMMIGRATION OFFICER/STAN LEE/BRITISH NARRATOR/
BOBBY/TOMMY/GROCERY BOY . . . . Paco Tolson

CHARACTERS

TONG
HUONG/THU/SAN/COP
QUANG/CHRIS
NHAN/THU'S BOYFRIEND/COWBOY/2ND GROCER
PLAYWRIGHT/LITTLE MAN
IMMIGRATION OFFICER/STAN LEE/ BRITISH NARRATOR
  BOBBY/TOMMY/GROCERY BOY

SETTING

El Dorado, Arkansas.

TIME

1980.

AUTHOR'S NOTES

Staging note

Three helpful hints when staging this show:

1. This play has a lot of scenes. Many of which are quite short. Because of that, the play works best when scenes "seamlessly transition" to the next without ever having to stop the show to reset furniture/props. Speed and velocity are your friends here.

2. The show walks a fine line between raucous comedy and touching drama. It literally goes from a puppet kung fu-training montage to a very real emotional breakup. The key to holding it all together is remembering that this is a play about six folks who desperately love each other but are not great at expressing that love.

3. Welcome to the *Vietgone* family. That's not really a staging note, just a thank you from me for reading/making this show.

SONG LIST

ACT ONE

ACT TWO

ACT ONE

0.

(A spotlight comes up on an actor playing the **PLAYWRIGHT**.*)*

PLAYWRIGHT. Hi, I'm playwright Qui Nguyen. I'm here to introduce you to my show *POOR YELLA REDNECKS*. But first, some pre-show announcements:

> *(The* **PLAYWRIGHT** *formally reads from a notecard.)*

Please silence all cellphones, the use of recording devices of any kind is strictly prohibited, in case of emergency please exit the door you just came in, and finally...this story is based on true events. All heavily researched. All one hundred percent historically accurate. Well, at least according to my mom. Now to begin our show, cue the single greatest narrator of all time from any medium!

> *(The* **PLAYWRIGHT** *and* **TONG** *walk into place as...)*

> *(A spotlight falls onto* **STAN LEE**.*)*

STAN LEE. *(Backed with superhero theme music.*)* Greetings, true believers, it's your old pal Stan Lee here – And right now, we are in the mysterious and marvelous land of El Dorado, Arkansas where our not-so-Far East hero currently conducts an interview with his immigrant mother for a play he is writing.

> *(***PLAYWRIGHT*** [thirties] sits across from his mother **TONG** [seventy] at a table. A tape recorder between them.)*

PLAYWRIGHT. So I want to interview you for a play that I'm writing.

TONG. Why?

PLAYWRIGHT. Because I think it'd be interesting to tell a story about how you built a life here in America as a Vietnamese refugee.

TONG. That a terrible idea.

PLAYWRIGHT. It's not terrible.

TONG. This is why you so poor.

PLAYWRIGHT. I'm not *so* poor.

TONG. No one want to hear story about old woman who speak bad English with bald son.

PLAYWRIGHT. I'm not bald.

TONG. Not yet.

PLAYWRIGHT. This isn't about me or my hairline.

TONG. Let me tell you what kind of story white people want to hear.

---

* A license to produce *Poor Yella Rednecks* does not include a performance license for any third-party or copyrighted music. Licensees should create an original composition or use music in the public domain. For further information, please see the Music and Third-Party Materials Use Note on page iii.

PLAYWRIGHT. Wait, why only "white people?"

TONG. Because only white people like to watch a play.

PLAYWRIGHT. All sorts of people watch plays, Mom.

TONG. Yes, all sorts of white people. It look like a Fleetwood Mac concert. It so white.

PLAYWRIGHT. Date: August 7, 2015

Interview with Tong Nguyen.

So when did you meet Dad?

TONG. *(Suddenly defensive.)* Why you want to talk about him?

PLAYWRIGHT. Because you both made me.

TONG. Only thing he made is trouble. I the one who made things work. That's all you need to know. Write that down.

PLAYWRIGHT. I need to know a little bit more than that if I'm gonna write a whole story about you.

TONG. Then maybe I don't want to dig up old history just so you can make a few dollar on play white people won't like.

PLAYWRIGHT. Then don't do it for "my play," do it for your grandkids: Sam and Felix – They love you.

You're their bà ngoai.

They'll want to know all this one day.

You won't be around forever.

Don't make them sad.

TONG. That is so manipulative.

Fine.

But before you write anything, I need to make some ground rule.

TONG. Rule number one: I don't want you to only tell happy thing.

PLAYWRIGHT. Why would I –

TONG. I see your other play. You like to write romantic and funny. But no life is all romance. And it is not all fun. Sometimes it is hard. We Vietnamese. We good at being hard. I want it to be true and hard.

PLAYWRIGHT. Fine.

> (**PLAYWRIGHT** *types a note into his computer, when he hits enter, we hear a... Ding!)*

> (**STAN LEE** *appears in the Playwright's home, uncomfortably close.)*

STAN LEE. Hey there, heroes, Stan Lee here, reminding all of you kids, no matter what you may see or hear today, this is a story that's *hard!*

> (**STAN LEE** *exits.)*

PLAYWRIGHT. Happy?

TONG. Rule number two: If this going to be my play, I want all the white people to sound like the way I hear them. Let them hear all the stupid stuff they say.

> *(Ding!)*

> (**TWO ASIAN ACTORS** *in "White Face" pop out from the wings.)*

WHITE GUY. Yeehaw! Get'er Done! I reckon!

WHITE GIRL. Catawampus! Kombucha! Woke!

WHITE GUY. *(As if proposing to her.)* Five dollar footlong!

WHITE GIRL. *(Hops into his arms.)* Hoochie Coochie!

> *(They exit.)*

TONG. And finally, I want to talk good. I want to talk like the way you talk.

PLAYWRIGHT. You sure about that? I got a fucking potty mouth.

TONG. Yes. I want a pot and a mouth. Like that.

PLAYWRIGHT. Alright.

(**PLAYWRIGHT** *types. Ding!*)

TONG. Can you do that motherfucking shit, motherfucker? Fuck yeah.

PLAYWRIGHT. So are we good? Can we start?

When did you meet Dad?

TONG. In 1975 – a little bit after I came to America.

PLAYWRIGHT. And where did you meet him?

TONG. A relocation camp in Fort Chaffee, Arkansas. Then we moved here to El Dorado six months later.

PLAYWRIGHT. Aw. So it really was "love at first sight."

TONG. Mm-hmm. And Santa Claus is real, as is the Easter Bunny, and capitalism works for everybody.

PLAYWRIGHT. You always told us it was love at first sight.

TONG. I know what we "told you."

PLAYWRIGHT. It wasn't –

TONG. You're a grown ass man. You know that shit ain't real.

PLAYWRIGHT. You weren't in love?

TONG. If you wanna call what we did "love," sure. We "loved" each other all over that camp. In bath stalls, in between the cabins, in our bunks, off our bunks, in other people's bunks.

PLAYWRIGHT. Oh God.

TONG. Calm down. When Saigon fell, I was separated from my little brother, your dad was separated from his first wife and kids. We were sad. We wanted to feel something other than –

PLAYWRIGHT. Wait. Hold up. What do you mean he was separated from his "first wife?"

> *(Beat.)*

TONG. What? I didn't say that.

PLAYWRIGHT. Dad was married before?

TONG. That's not really my story to tell.

PLAYWRIGHT. MOM!

TONG. Fine. Yes. Your dad was married when we met. Thus some of our problems. But he didn't make it any better.

PLAYWRIGHT. What happened to her?

TONG. Same thing that happened to a lot of Vietnamese families. He escaped, she didn't. So he ended up here where I met him. We were heartbroken. So we comforted each other...with our crotches.

Which eventually led him to do something incredibly stupid...

PLAYWRIGHT. *(Announces to the audience.)* 1975.

El Dorado, Arkansas.

> **(TONG** *[seventy] transforms into* **TONG** *[thirties] before our very eyes.)*
>
> *(Projection: 1975.)*
>
> *(Projection: El Dorado, Arkansas.)*
>
> **(TONG** *walks over and joins* **QUANG** *[thirties].)*

(They pass a joint between them.)

QUANG. I have a great idea.

(Inhales.)

Wait for it.

(Exhales.)

We should get cheeseburgers.

(Weed cough.)

And married.

TONG. Wait. Are you serious?

QUANG. Well, I am hungry.

TONG. No, stupid, about getting married.

QUANG. Why would I be joking?

TONG. One, you're stoned –

QUANG. No, you're stoned.

TONG. – Two, it's Tuesday, the least romantic day of the week. And three, you still kinda got a wife and I still kinda got a boyfriend.

QUANG. You haven't broken up with Bobby?

TONG. Shut up, he's really hard to dump. He's like the nicest dude I ever dated...unlike you, who's an asshole.

QUANG. I'm not an asshole.

TONG. You're about to ghost your wife for your sidepiece. That's not a thing nice guys do.

QUANG. She's there. I'm here. If she thinks I'm dead, she can move on. I gotta do the same.

TONG. Aw, that's like the most romantic thing you've ever said to me. I've always wanted to be someone's sloppy seconds.

QUANG. You know you're way more than that.

TONG. Yeah, whatever.

QUANG. I'm serious. I got married to Thu because I was running off to die in a war. I was doing what I thought I was supposed to do. But you and me...well, I ain't here because I'm worried about dying. I'm with you because I'm ready to live.

TONG. You are so fucking corny.

[MUSIC NO. 01 – PROPOSAL]

QUANG. You. Me. A starry night sky to dream under. If I got you, I got everything I need.

(Rapped.)

I KNOW YOU THINK I'M JOKIN'
WHAT THE HELL AM I SMOKIN'?
BUT BEING NEXT TO YOU IS WHAT'S GOT MY HEART
    THUMPIN'
OUR KIDDIES WILL BE CUTIES,
BRING OVER THAT FINE BOOTIE
NOTHING'S GONNA STOP US WITH OUR COMBINED
    BEAUTY

TONG.

YOU REALLY ARE SO CORNY

QUANG.

YEAH, YOU THE ONE FOR ME

TONG.

I JUST LIKE YOUR BODY
IT MAKES ME KINDA HORNY

QUANG.

KEEP ON DENYIN'
I SEE THE WAY YOU SMILIN'

TONG.

IT'S ONLY 'CAUSE I'M STONED
MY MIND IS FRIKKEN FLYIN'

QUANG.

> WE MAKE A GOOD TEAM THO
> TOGETHER WE'RE SPECIAL
> WE'LL TACKLE THIS COUNTRY
> PULL OFF THE IMPOSSIBLE
> LOVE WILL BE OUR BACKBONE
> WE'LL MAKE THIS PLACE OUR NEW HOME
> WE'LL DO IT WITH EASE AS WE MARCH THROUGH THE
>   UNKNOWN
> WHERE THE HELL ARE WE GOING?
> WE DON'T KNOW BUT WE KNOWING
> HOWEVER IMPOSSIBLE THIS IS
> WE'LL MAKE THIS PLACE OUR NEW HOMELAND
> HOME
> WE'LL MAKE IT HOME

TONG.

> THIS SHIT IS KINDA SCARY
> I'M NOT THE TYPE TO MARRY

QUANG.

> THERE'S NOTHING TO FEAR
> TOGETHER WE'RE EXTR'ORDINARY

TONG.

> YOU'RE FUCKING UP MY GAME PLAN
> WHY CAN'T YA JUST BE COOL, MAN?
> SUPPOSED TO BE A LAY BUT THIS LAY HAS GOTTEN OUTTA
>   HAND

QUANG.

> I GET IT, PRETTY BABY
> I KNOW THIS SOUNDS CRAZY
> BUT YOU AND I SO DAMN FLY
> WE SHOULD BE MARRIED
> OUR LIFE WILL BE AMAZING
> WE'LL ROCK THIS NEW NATION
> WE'LL MAKE ALL THAT MOOLAH

QUANG.

WE'LL BE CRAZY RICH ASIANS
ONE DAY WE'RE GONNA THRIVE IN THIS FOREIGN LAND
BUT TODAY WE'RE GONNA DO WHATEVER WE CAN
TO CREATE A PLACE WHERE WE BOTH CAN STAND
DEFYING ALL THE HATERS WHO SAY WE CAN'T
WHERE THE HELL ARE WE GOING?
WE DON'T KNOW BUT WE KNOWING
HOWEVER IMPOSSIBLE THIS IS
WE'LL MAKE THIS PLACE OUR NEW HOMELAND

TONG.

HOME
WE'LL MAKE IT HOME
I WANNA SAY YES, BUT I GOTTA CONFESS
I'M NOT THE TYPE INT'RESTED IN BEING POSSESSED
I WON'T TAKE NO LIP,
I WON'T POUR NO TEA
IF YOU LOOKING FOR THAT BITCH
WELL, THAT BITCH AIN'T ME

QUANG.

SO WILL YOU MARRY ME?

TONG.

YA YOU FUCKED IN THE HEAD

QUANG.

ONLY FOR YOU BABY
ARE WE GONNA GET WED?

TONG.

YOUR ASS IS STILL MARRIED,
MY ASS STILL A MESS

QUANG.

I WANT YOU FOREVER –

TONG.

FUCK IT, MY ANSWER IS YES

QUANG.
STEP BACK SUCKER
CAN'T BELIEVE YOU JUST SAID IT

TONG.
BETTER PUT A RING ON IT
YOU CAN FUCKING FORGET IT

QUANG.
TOGETHER FOREVER
THIS SHIT'LL BE EPIC

TONG.
WE'RE GONNA GET MARRIED
CAN'T BELIEVE I JUST SAID IT

QUANG.
WHERE THE HELL ARE WE GOING?

TONG.
WE DON'T KNOW BUT WE KNOWING

QUANG.
HOWEVER IMPOSSIBLE THIS IS

TONG.
WE'LL MAKE THIS PLACE OUR NEW HOMELAND

TONG & QUANG.
HOME
WE'LL MAKE IT HOME
WHERE THE HELL ARE WE GOING?
WE DON'T KNOW BUT WE KNOWING
HOWEVER IMPOSSIBLE THIS IS
WE'LL MAKE THIS PLACE OUR NEW HOMELAND
HOME
WE'LL MAKE IT HOME

(They kiss.)

(The **PLAYWRIGHT** *walks in.)*

PLAYWRIGHT. Aw, that's cute. However, as my mom stated previously, this is not a love story. It's the story about surviving one.

1.

(Projection: Five years later...)

PLAYWRIGHT. Fast forward.

Five years later... 1980, El Dorado, Arkansas...

Inside a quaint trailer, we find my sweet kind-hearted grandmother enjoying some light American entertainment.

(Lights up on **HUONG** *[sixty-five] smoking cigarettes, watching a '70s sitcom.*)*

A TV VOICE-OVER. *(To a '70s sitcom theme.)*
MINDLESS HOLLYWOOD TUBE
SUZANNE SOMERS' BIG BOOBS
COMMERCIAL BREAKS, LOSE WEIGHT, TITS FAKE
POLYAMORY'S COOL...

HUONG. *(Turns off TV.)* Well, this is dumb as fuck.

(There's noise at the front door. **HUONG** *pulls out a knife.)*

I HAVE A KNIFE, ASSHOLE!

*(***TONG** *[now thirty-six] enters with a waitress apron and three styrofoam containers of food in hand.)*

TONG. Hey Mom.

HUONG. You're late.

TONG. How was Little Man today?

---

* A license to produce *Poor Yella Rednecks* does not include a performance license for any third-party or copyrighted music, recordings or images. Licensees must acquire rights for any copyrighted recordings or images or create their own.

HUONG. I ate him.

TONG. Not funny.

HUONG. What's not funny is how hungry I am. What took you so long?

TONG. They let go of Daisy this morning –

HUONG. What? Paul fired Daisy?! What happened?

TONG. He's getting old and the diner isn't making the money it used to and…you clearly don't give a crap.

HUONG. Nope. What I care about is dinner and it's already past ten.

(**HUONG** *goes for the styrofoam containers.*)

TONG. Quang home?

HUONG. He's out getting drunk with that dummy friend of his that's moving to Texas. God, that man is pretty.

TONG. Don't talk about my husband like that.

HUONG. I'm not.

TONG. Ew. Nhan's worse. He's a perv that would sleep with anything.

HUONG. Really?

TONG. No, Mom. NO.

(**HUONG** *digs into her food.*)

HUONG. Whenever you get fired from Paul's, could your next place of employment be somewhere that actually serves something edible?

TONG. I'm not getting fired.

HUONG. There's a few things in this world that I know. One, I look incredible for a woman my age. And two, my oldest daughter is a terrible employee.

TONG. I'm not a terrible –

HUONG. What happened at your last job?

TONG. They had to downsize.

HUONG. Yeah, downsize to less people who slap their bosses.

TONG. He slapped my ass, I slapped his face. Fair's fair.

HUONG. And inevitably when you lose your shit at Paul or someone at Paul's, can your next job be at Oriental Gardens? Their chicken lo mein is delightful.

TONG. How was Little Man today?

HUONG. He's fine. He went to school. I fed him. He's asleep. It's like I've raised kids before.

TONG. Trust me, Mom. You're not great at it.

HUONG. You only think that because you now see how white people do it.

TONG. You pulled me out of school because – quote – "pretty girls don't need school."

HUONG. And I'm right. What's school done for you?

TONG. Education matters.

HUONG. Shut up. You're skinny and pretty. That's what matters. Especially here where everyone's fat and looks fifteen years older than their actual age. School can't teach you this. This is what you need to take care of your family.

TONG. So you want me to become a hooker now?

HUONG. No, dummy. What you need is to use those looks to get a better man.

TONG. I have a good man.

HUONG. I didn't say a good man, I said a better man. Quang's handsome, but he can't even get a full-time job.

TONG. That's not his fault.

HUONG. I know it's not. It's this place's fault.

TONG. Quang's doing fine. We're going to be fine. We've been saving up. We have a plan.

HUONG. That's funny. I have a plan too.

(**HUONG** *pulls out an old cigar box filled with photos and hands* **TONG** *one of them.*)

TONG. Who the hell is it this time?

HUONG. Tam Vu's son. He does nails. In Shreveport. That's his number on the back.

TONG. I'm not leaving Quang. I'm not moving to Shreveport. I'm not hooking up with a dude who does nails.

(**QUANG** *and* **NHAN** [*thirties*] *come in.*)

QUANG. Hello everyone.

NHAN. What's up, fam!

ALL. Nhan!

TONG. Hey babe.

(**QUANG** *and* **TONG** *kiss.*)

I thought you two would be out drinking.

QUANG. We are.

NHAN. *(Shows bag full of beers.)* Best bar in town.

QUANG. Ain't no rednecks gonna give us shit here.

HUONG. *(To* **QUANG**.*)* Yeah but now we have to put up with your dumb ass.

QUANG. *(Dripping with sarcasm.)* God, I love your mom. She's like Charles Manson, but meaner.

(To **TONG**.*)* You thirsty?

TONG. *(With a wink.)* Not for beer.

HUONG. Oh God.

NHAN. Okay, we get it, you love each other.

TONG. Whatever. Shut up.

HUONG. Throw me one.

> (**NHAN** *hands her a beer. They crack them open and chug like frat boys.*)

TONG. This is nice. Fancy. Real classy.

> (**NHAN** *and* **HUONG** *slam their beers down simultaneously.*)

NHAN. Damn, your mom's hardcore.

TONG. Don't encourage her.

HUONG. You can encourage me all you want, big boy.

QUANG. So Nhan wants me to go down to Houston next week.

NHAN. That's right. HOUSTON!

QUANG. He wants a wingman to help him check out his new city.

NHAN. Not that I need a wingman. I can pick up girls on my own.

HUONG. Prove it.

TONG. Mom, stop!

QUANG. So do you wanna come with me?

NHAN. Bro, you're inviting Tong to come along?

TONG. Don't be jealous.

NHAN. I'm not jealous. Why would I be jealous?

HUONG. We could make them both jealous.

(**HUONG** *reaches for* **NHAN**, *but* **TONG** *intercepts.*)

TONG. *(To* **HUONG**.*)* Sit down.

(**TONG** *grabs the mail off a kitchen counter.*)

Watching Nhan crash and burn in a new area code could be entertaining, I'll ask for the time off.

(**TONG** *flips through the envelopes and then stops at one.*)

Is this airmail?

HUONG. Must be from your brother. He probably needs money.

TONG. It's not from Saigon. It's from Soc Trang, Quang's hometown.

(**TONG** *hands* **QUANG** *the envelope.*)

It's from your wife.

QUANG. That's impossible.

TONG. Clearly it isn't.

QUANG. What does this mean?

(*Ka-chunk! Lights suddenly come up on an* **IMMIGRATION OFFICER** *as he looks at the letter.*)

(**TONG** *and* **QUANG** *watch the* **IMMIGRATION OFFICER** *examine the parcel.*)

TONG. He's nodding his head an awful lot. That must be a good sign, right?

IMMIGRATION OFFICER. Get'er done, Tucker Carlson, G.O.P.

TONG. Or bad. Really bad.

IMMIGRATION OFFICER. Mister Quang, in land of Cheeseburger, Batman can no have two Robins. Only one bat to one bird. Maybe at Panda Express, General Tso's Chicken can have many sides, but not at Burger King. Burger King can only get one French Fry.

TONG. Okay. So Quang can't be married to two people. Whatever. How'd his ex find him in the first place?

(*The* **IMMIGRATION OFFICER** *shrugs.*)

A shrug? That's helpful. Did you go to college to learn that shrug?

IMMIGRATION OFFICER. Please chill pill, my awesome blossom. Me no see such item on menu, but you having much bigger Main Event on Pay-Per-View.

QUANG. What problem?

IMMIGRATION OFFICER. BIG main event.

QUANG. Fine. "Big problem." What is it?

(*The* **IMMIGRATION OFFICER** *looks at both* **QUANG** *and* **TONG**, *takes a deep breath, and tells them:*)

IMMIGRATION OFFICER. Get ready... It's a showstopper... Sunny Bono's going solo.

TONG. What!

QUANG. What do you mean "Tong's not my wife anymore?"

IMMIGRATION OFFICER. Only one french fry, potato chip. And Tong not that French Fry. Quang's only French Fry is Quang's first French Fry.

TONG. Then what do we do?

IMMIGRATION OFFICER. Quang and first French Fry must have series finale. Only then can Quang and Tong have spinoff.

QUANG. How long does that take?

IMMIGRATION OFFICER. An Infinite Jest.

And until that last page, Tong is Tong, Quang is Quang. No crossovers.

(The **IMMIGRATION OFFICER** *disappears.)*

TONG. Whatever. I knew you were married when we got together. Something like this was bound to happen.

QUANG. Hey, I'll talk to a lawyer and settle things with Thu. I'll fix this.

TONG. I know you will.

I should get to work.

I'll see you at home.

> *(***TONG** *gives* **QUANG** *a kiss and leaves.)*

> *(***QUANG** *stares at the letter his first wife sent him. He reads it. As he does…)*

> *(***THU** *[thirty-five] appears. She's dressed beautifully in a traditional Vietnamese ao dai. Her face is warm. She has a huge smile.)*

[MUSIC NO. 02 – LEMME REINTRODUCE MYSELF]

> *(A beat drops. After the first line,* **THU***'s smile disappears as she goes hard.)*

THU. *(Rapped.)*
> LET ME REINTRODUCE MYSELF
> I'M BETTER KNOWN AS THAT SHORTY THAT YOU UP AND
>   LEFT
> I MUST BE CRAZY, BABY
> THOUGHT YOU WERE DEAD
> WE THREW A FUNERAL TO COMMEMORATE YOUR DEATH
> BUT NOW I'M WRITING YOU,
> WHAT THE HELL, YOU ALIVE???
> THE HELL HAVE YOU BEEN THIS WHOLE GODDAMN
>   TIME?
> AS I RECALL, BABY, YOU'D STAY BY MY SIDE
> BUT I DON'T SEE YOU HERE, I MUSTA GONE BLIND

THU.
MUST BE IT, BABY, 'CAUSE YOU NEVER WOULD LIE
YA PROMISED ME THE WORLD TO ALWAYS BE MINE
I'M A FUCKING IDIOT FOR BUYING THOSE LINES
BUT THAT'S OKAY, BABY, GOT A NEW GUY BY MY SIDE

(Lights up on **THU'S BOYFRIEND.***)*

AND I GOTTA SAY, BABY, HE'S MUCH BETTER THAN YOU
AND WHAT HE'S PACKING LOW,
HE'S MUCH BIGGER THAN YOU
AND IN THE BEDROOM,
A BETTER LOVER THAN YOU
BUT MOST IMPORTANTLY,
HE'S MAD RICHER THAN YOU
BUT NOW THAT I FOUND YOU, GUESS WHAT HE SAID?
HE WAS GONNA PROPOSE, BUT YELLED –

THU'S BOYFRIEND.
FUCK YOU!

THU.
– AND LEFT!
HE DOESN'T WANT A LADY WHOSE MAN'S STILL AROUND
WHY COULDN'T YOU BE COOL AND STAY DEAD IN THE
    GROUND?
SO WHEN THEY ASK ABOUT YOU,
YOUR DAUGHTER, YOUR SON
DON'T THINK IMMA HOLD BACK MY MOTHERFUCKIN'
    TONGUE
IMMA TELL THEM THE TRUTH
YO, YOUR DAD'S A FUCKIN' BUM
WHEN SHIT GETS HAIRY, HE UP AND RUNS
SO FUCK YOU, BABY, FUCK ALL THAT YOU SAID
FUCK EV'RY MEMORY SINCE THE DAY WE BOTH MET
FUCK YOU, BABY, FUCK ALL THAT YOU ARE
FUCK EV'RY GODDAMN THING YOU DONE SINCE THE WAR
FUCK YOU, BABY, FUCK ALL THAT YOU'LL BE
FUCK YOUR NEW HOMELAND FROM SEA TO SHINING SEA

THU.
> FUCK YOU, BABY, FUCK THIS MOMENT RIGHT NOW
> CUZ I'M DONE WRITING YOU. FUCK OFF. I'M OUT.

2.

(Cut to…)

(A drunk **BRITISH NARRATOR** *[complete with problematic pith hat] enters.)*

BRITISH NARRATOR. Good day. Pardon me. *Excusez-moi.*

Hello there, I am Classic British Narrator, and I'm here to introduce you to a day in the life of an Asian waitress living in El Dorado, Arkansas.

Behold! The Asian waitress in her natural environment: cleaning tables at a local diner.

(Lights up on **TONG** *cleaning up a table.)*

As you can see, it's a thankless job, a tedious job. But it's a job nonetheless, one the Asian waitress is grateful to have. But having a job is one thing, keeping it is another. Behold a cowboy of the deep southern persuasion.

(A **COWBOY** *enters.)*

COWBOY. Howdy.

BRITISH NARRATOR. He notices the Asian waitress from across the way. His eyes transfixed on her slender figure. His internal pride and caucasian privilege inspire him to approach with abandon –

(The **COWBOY** *"trips" and slaps* **TONG** *on the ass.)*

TONG. HEY!

COWBOY. Howdy, sweetpea. People's Court my digits on your J-Lo.

BRITISH NARRATOR. Translation: Greetings to you, attractive female person! Apologies on my hand accidentally grazing your aesthetically-pleasing posterior.

TONG. Don't "howdy" me, asshole.

COWBOY. Egg roll, Hook 'em Horns!

BRITISH NARRATOR. My lady of Far Eastern descent, you seem upset.

COWBOY. Weight watchers, eggplant. Booty call?

BRITISH NARRATOR. Let me make it up to you by offering you a vegetable dinner service within my trousers.

COWBOY. Chopped salad, Egg roll. Red solo cup?

BRITISH NARRATOR. What do you say, Asian lady? Do you wish to party?

> (**TONG** *steps to the* **COWBOY**.)

What our lovely leading lady wishes would have happened...

TONG. Sure. Let's party.

> (**TONG** *picks up a fork and tosses it.*)

> (*It slams into the* **COWBOY**'s *face, killing him.*)

> (*Blackout.*)

> (*Reset.*)

BRITISH NARRATOR. What she really wishes would have happened...

COWBOY. Chopped salad, Egg roll. Red solo cup?

TONG. Yeah, you know I'd love to, but –

> (**QUANG** *flies in and Superman-punches the* **COWBOY** *–)*

QUANG. *(Confidently states.)* Fuck my ex-wife. Fuck those other kids. I only want you...and now I'm rich!

> *(He rips off his shirt, grabs* **TONG***, and they furiously start making out.)*

> *(Blackout.)*

> *(Reset.)*

BRITISH NARRATOR. And finally...

TONG. What actually happened.

COWBOY. Chopped salad, Egg roll. Red Solo Cup?

TONG. Yeah. Fuck you, asshole.

> *(***TONG*** slaps him!)*

COWBOY. *(Runs away.)* Mitch McConnell!

BRITISH NARRATOR. Exotic and erotic!

3.

*(**HUONG** fills a metal children's lunchbox.)*

HUONG. Little Man! We have to go! Where are you?

LITTLE MAN. *(Offstage.)* I don't want to go, Bà Ngoai..

(A ball rolls onstage.)

HUONG. What do you mean you don't want to go? It's school. You have to go. "Education matters."

> *(**HUONG** rolls the ball back to the unseen* **LITTLE MAN.***)*

LITTLE MAN. No one talks to me there.

HUONG. That's not true. People talk to you.

What about those fat kids you were playing with yesterday?

> *(**LITTLE MAN** finally appears from behind a couch, now holding the ball. He's played by a super cute puppet – made of felt, fuzzy hair – the kind of puppet that makes the audience say "aw" as soon as he appears [Think Disney, not banraku].)*

LITTLE MAN. They took my Spiderman. I was chasing them to get it back. I then got yelled at for hitting Tommy Gathright cause he said I should go back to China.

HUONG. Well, Tommy's stupid. You're obviously not Chinese. The Chinese are awful people. Almost as bad as the French.

> *(**LITTLE MAN** won't make eye contact.)*

Is that why you hit him?

*(**LITTLE MAN** nods.)*

LITTLE MAN. He said I shouldn't be here. He said Mom and Dad should have stayed wherever they came from. He said they should have all died there. That's why I hit Tommy. Was that bad?

(A beat.)

Grandma?

HUONG. No, it's not bad that you hit him – it's GREAT that you hit him. Let me give you some advice, next time Tommy gives you any lip, knock his dumb ass out, stomp on his neck, and spit in his ugly fat face. Do you understand?

(Beat.)

LITTLE MAN. No.

HUONG. Just...don't do it again, okay? I'll make sure your mom talks to your teacher about it. Now go grab an umbrella, it's raining outside.

LITTLE MAN. Yes, Grandma.

*(**LITTLE MAN** walks away.)*

HUONG. Hey.

LITTLE MAN. Yes, Grandma?

HUONG. You're a good kid. Way better than any of those dummies on the playground. Mommy and Grandma will get it fixed.

LITTLE MAN. Okay, Grandma.

*(Once he's out of the room, **HUONG** looks up to the heavens.)*

HUONG. Mu! You hear me up there? I wish I could join you already because this place sucks!

4.

(**QUANG**, *alone, with a pen a paper. He's writing a letter to his ex.*)

[MUSIC NO. 3 – GIMME A CHANCE]

QUANG. *(Rapped.)*
I LIVE WITH REGRET
I KNOW THAT ME LIVING MUST FUCK WITH YOUR HEAD
I THOUGHT THIS WAS BEST
THAT YOU'D MOVE ON IF YOU THOUGHT I WAS DEAD,
BUT NOW I'M A MESS
WHAT'S HAPPENED TO YOU IS NOT WHAT I MEANT,
BUT I GOTTA EXPRESS
I WISH I WAS STRONG,
I THOUGHT I WAS STRONG,
BUT WHEN THE TIME CAME I FLED FROM SAIGON
I RAN AWAY CUZ OF THE V.C.
AFRAID THEY'D TORTURE AND KILL ME
DIDN'T REALIZE IT'D COST ME MY FAM'LY
I HAVE A NEW FAM'LY
I KNOW YOU HATE ME
THIS SITCH WE'RE IN IS INSANITY
IT'S A TRAGEDY, A CALAMITY
I KNOW THAT MY KIDS THERE MUST HATE ME SO BADLY
AND THAT'S ON ME
I'M NOW IN A PLACE WHERE NO ONE SEES ME
TRAPPED IN THE LAND OF THE GREEDY
NOT SEEN AS A MAN, BUT A REFUGEE
WHAT'S LEFT OF ME IS JUST AGONY
I PRETEND TO SMILE BUT I'M WEARY
NOW I FIN'LY SEE CLEARLY
THIS LAND OF THE FREE IS A THEORY
WITH NO ROOM FOR ME

NO VIETNAMESE

QUANG.
I WISH I COULD FIX THE ISSUES
AND PAIN THAT YOU'RE WRESTLING WITH
I FEEL SO DAMN SICK
I KNOW THAT WE'RE OVER BUT I STILL LOVE MY KIDS
THEY ARE STILL IT,
THE BEST PART OF ME THAT'S NOT FULL OF SHIT
I GOTTA ADMIT
I'M SO AFRAID,
SO GODDAMN AFRAID
I MIGHT BE ALIVE BUT I LOST MY DAMN WAY
SO GIMME A CHANCE,
ONE FINAL CHANCE
TO PROVE TO MYSELF I CAN STILL BE THEIR DAD,
TO FIN'LY BE MORE THAN THIS BROKEN ASS MAN
JUST GIVE ME A CHANCE,
THAT'S ALL THAT I ASK,
SO I CAN SAY TO MYSELF I'M STILL A MAN,
NOT JUST A GHOST IN THIS FOREIGN LAND

(Sings.)

JUST GIMME A CHANCE
JUST ONE LAST CHANCE
JUST GIMME A CHANCE
GIMMIE ONE LAST CHANCE
JUST GIMME ONE LAST CHANCE
ONE. LAST. CHANCE.

*(As the song ends, **QUANG** puts the letter into an envelope and gets back to work.)*

*(**NHAN** runs onstage, freaked out.)*

NHAN. Quang! QUANG!

QUANG. Holy shit, man, what the fuck??

(**NHAN** *catches his breath.*)

NHAN. Just...phew!

I'm about to head out of town and wanted to catch ya before you headed to work.

QUANG. That's pretty easy to do considering I don't got a job.

NHAN. What happened to building sheds for Jimmy?

QUANG. He ended up hiring –

NHAN. A white guy?

QUANG. Yeah.

NHAN. Bro, I don't know how you do it, it's like this town is trying to keep you poor.

QUANG. I'm not poor.

NHAN. You might not be third-world flies-flying-around-your-mouth poor, but still – you broke.

QUANG. I'm not broke. I'm...pre-rich.

NHAN. Uh-huh.

QUANG. I'll find something.

NHAN. You know, bro, there are options. You could move with me to Houston.

QUANG. Yeah, I don't see that happening.

NHAN. Lemme ask you somethin'. Have you ever seen a yella fella in a cowboy hat? Cuz in Texas, cowboy hats. Ladies *love* that shit.

QUANG. I got a girl.

NHAN. That's not the point. There, you're seen.

Just think about it, you could hop onto the back of my bike and the next thing you know –

NHAN. *(Rapped.)*

> YELLA MOTHERFUCKERS ON A MOTORCYCLE
> RIDING ALL NIGHT 'TIL OUR ARRIVAL
> NOT STOPPING, BRO, 'TIL WE HIT TEXAS,
> 'CAUSE HOUSTON IS THE SPOT WHERE THEY RESPECT
> US –

QUANG. Okay, okay, I get the hard sell.

NHAN. Ya gotta admit it does sound fun, right? Right?

QUANG. It doesn't sound bad, but –

NHAN. Seriously, man, there's a community being built down there. A community that appreciates who we are and what we've done. You were a Captain in the South Vietnamese Air Force, that'll get you respect there. Unlike here, where all these assholes just think you're some dumb immigrant and won't hire you for shit. Or am I wrong?

> *(**QUANG** contemplates the idea.)*

QUANG. Tong won't wanna move.

NHAN. That's when you gotta drop the hammer, man. Tell her "I am a Vietnamese man, this is a Vietnamese household, what I say is LAW!"

QUANG. I see why you're still single.

NHAN. She really love this place that much?

QUANG. No, but she really hates relocating her life that much. We've all had more than our fair share at saying our good-byes. She's just done with that shit, ya know?

NHAN. Yeah, I know, I just... I'm gonna miss seeing you all the time.

QUANG. I'm gonna see you this weekend.

> *(**QUANG** gives **NHAN** a friendly punch on his arm.)*

QUANG. Hey... I need you to do me a favor. I hear there's people in Houston that can get money to Vietnam.

(**QUANG** *pulls cash out of his wallet and his letter.*)

NHAN. Whoa. Where'd you get this?

QUANG. It's my savings. Five thousand dollars. When you get to Houston, I want you to send this to Thu and my kids.

(**NHAN** *gives him look.*)

It was Tong's idea...

(**NHAN**'*s not buying it.*)

Okay, I'll tell her later. But she'll be okay with it. Tong's cool. Super cool. So...can you do this for me?

NHAN. (*Nods.*) You can count on me.

(*They hug.*)

I love you, man.

QUANG. Love you too, bro.

(**NHAN** *doesn't let go.*)

You can let go now.

NHAN. Shhh. No more words. Just emotion.

5.

(**TONG** *enters her home.*)

HUONG. You're home early.

TONG. I talked to Little Man's teachers.

HUONG. Good. I don't like my grandson getting shit.

TONG. I like that you like him, Mom, but –

HUONG. Don't get excited. He's the only one that I can actually stand here.

TONG. Little Man's right, no one really talks to him at school. Including his teacher. They don't know what to do with him.

(*Beat.*)

They want to hold him back.

HUONG. What? No. Fuck that.

TONG. They had some good / reasons.

HUONG. They're assholes.

TONG. They're just teachers, Mom, / who are trying their best.

HUONG. They're shitty ass / shit teachers.

TONG. They're not shitty teachers.

HUONG. You yelled at them, right? Tell me you yelled at them. 'Cause I'm gonna go down there and do me some yelling. And my English is shit so I'm gonna come off crazy...which will probably help me get my point across.

TONG. They're holding him back because they don't understand him.

HUONG. He's five. No one understands any fucking five year old.

TONG. This is different.

HUONG. This is bullshit. They need to get better at doing their jobs and not blame my grandson for their shortcomings.

TONG. All he knows is Vietnamese. All they know is English. How do you expect them to teach him?

HUONG. They could learn Vietnamese?

TONG. This is serious, Mom. If he can't speak English, he can't be taught. He needs to be fully immersed.

HUONG. What's that supposed to mean?

TONG. They recommend we stop speaking Vietnamese to him at home. Only English.

HUONG. How am I supposed to talk to him?

TONG. He's not hearing English enough to learn it, Mom. He only gets a few hours of it at school. That's not enough. Can you just help me for once?

HUONG. Help you do what exactly? Help you make my grandson more like them and less like me?

TONG. I'm trying to give him a future. We live here. We're not going back. If he can't talk like them, all he gets to be is an unemployed waitress in a trailer park.

HUONG. This is fucked.

TONG. He's my son. It's my responsibility to do all I can to help him thrive even if that means we have to sacrifice some things.

HUONG. What you're asking me to sacrifice is a relationship with my grandson. If he doesn't understand me, how will he ever get to know me?

TONG. That's not true. You're his bà ngoai.. / He loves you.

HUONG. Sure, I'm his grandma. But what happens when he learns English so well that he doesn't think in Vietnamese anymore? Huh? What then? What happens when his insides no longer match mine? What happens when he looks at me the same way the people here look at me? Like I'm less. Like I'm invisible. I'm supposed to turn him into a stranger just so he can do good at school?

TONG. No one said turn him into a stranger.

HUONG. You're right. You want something worse – you want me to turn him white.

TONG. That's not –

HUONG. I'm not gonna do it! NO!

(**HUONG** *storms out as* **QUANG** *enters.*)

QUANG. What's that about?

TONG. Don't worry about it. We have something more important to talk about.

QUANG. Yeah, I wanted to talk to you about something as well.

TONG. I have some good news! I'm losing my job.

QUANG. What?

TONG. Paul said I have until the end of the month.

QUANG. What happened?

TONG. I slapped a customer today, but that has nothing to do with me losing my job.

Paul's retiring. He's closing shop. He's old, the customers aren't coming in like they used to – so he's shutting down Paul's Dairy Diner and moving on.

QUANG. How's this good news?

TONG. Because I have a plan. We have five thousand dollars. Maybe instead of buying a house, maybe we put in an offer for the diner.

QUANG. What? Why?

TONG. So we could have it. I would run it. You would work there. It'd be ours. We would be our own bosses.

We could slap whoever we want. I even have a name: East Main Dairy Diner…because it's on East Main and we're from the East.

QUANG. Do you even know how to cook?

TONG. It's American food. Pancakes, french fries, burgers. You either dip it in grease or lay it in grease. It's not that hard.

QUANG. The hours. You'd never be home.

TONG. We'd make that diner our home.

Five thousand dollars is enough to make a deposit. Paul's our friend, he might actually go for it. We'd be making our own destiny, creating our own kingdom. What do you think?

QUANG. I think…it's irresponsible.

TONG. How's it irresponsible?

QUANG. I think it's a really dumb way to spend our money.

Restaurants are a really risky business. Especially early on when no one knows who you are –

TONG. Sure, but the diner already has a built in clientele. And the only reason why Paul was losing customers at all is because he kept closing early because he was tired. I'm not tired. I'm thirty-five. And Paul would show us what to do. He's a good guy. We could do this.

QUANG. We're saving for a house.

TONG. A house can wait.

QUANG. NO. We're saving for a house. We're not touching that money. We worked too hard. It's too important to just spend it on a whim.

TONG. This isn't a –

QUANG. This discussion is over.

TONG. Whoa, what do you mean "this discussion is over."

QUANG. I'm saying there's nothing to talk about. We're not buying a diner. We're Vietnamese. Vietnamese don't buy diners.

TONG. So suddenly what you say is law now? When the fuck did we agree to that?

QUANG. *(Tries out Nhan's words.)* I'm a Vietnamese man. This is a Vietnamese household. I get to make these calls.

(A tense beat.)

TONG. What was that?

QUANG. *(Realizing he fucked up.)* I'm sorry, that came out wrong.

TONG. Yeah, FUCK YOU! I didn't get married to some "Vietnamese man" to be in any "Vietnamese household."

QUANG. I'm sorry. That was wrong of me, it's just – look, if you really want to do something drastic right now... how about we move to Texas?

TONG. Move to Texas?

QUANG. Nhan says there's a good community there.

TONG. I don't want to be in fucking Texas.

QUANG. Don't you miss being around other Vietnamese?

TONG. I miss being in Vietnam, yes. But being around other Vietnamese here in America only reminds me of one thing: that I'm not actually in Vietnam anymore. Where my brother is. Where his wife is. And his two boys who I've never met – who I have no idea if I'll ever meet – so NO I don't want to move to some Vietnamese community right now.

QUANG. Okay, maybe we should take a moment and chill.

TONG. Yeah, let's chill. Maybe you should go to Texas this weekend without me.

QUANG. I don't want that.

TONG. But maybe I do. Maybe we both need to figure some shit out separately.

QUANG. What's that supposed to mean?

TONG. It means this is a lot harder than I thought it was going to be, Quang. I need some space to think.

QUANG. Think about what exactly?

TONG. I just need some space. Away from my "Vietnamese man" and his "Vietnamese household."

(Awkward silence.)

QUANG. This is fucked. You want me to go alone. Fine. I'll go. And I'm going to have a GREAT time.

TONG. I hope you do. Maybe I will too.

QUANG. *(Oh shit.)* What?

TONG. You do you.

*(**QUANG** leaves the house, slamming the door.)*

*(**TONG** goes to sit on the couch to sulk, realizes she's sitting on Huong's cigar box of potential suitors.)*

*(**TONG** takes a peek inside it.)*

(She then opens it and peruses.)

(An idea hits, she picks up the phone and dials.)

(On phone.) Hi. This is Tong. Would you be interested in dinner?

6.

(Projection: HOUSTON, TEXAS.)

[MUSIC NO. 04 – HOUSTON]

(Huge lights and sound.)

*(A beat drops as **NHAN** walks **QUANG** through the club.)*

ALL. Hey!

NHAN. *(Rapped)*
WELCOME TO HOUSTON, VIET CAPITOL OF TEXAS
WHATEVER YA WANT, SON,
YOU KNOW THAT WE GOT THAT HOMESTYLE FRESHNESS
    THAT YA NEED
FROM BOWLS OF HOT PHO TO YUMMY BANH MI!
OUR GIRLIES ARE FLY, THE HOMIES ARE SLY
WE PARTY ALL NIGHT,
WE KEEP OUR SHIT SUPER TIGHT
SLICK RHYTHM BEATS FLOWING – WE VIETNAMESE
WE ALL DIF'RENT BLOOD, BUT WE FAMILY!
SO THROW ON YOUR SMOOTH SHIT,
YOU KNOW YOU WAN' DO THIS
WE KICKIN' A.Z.N.'S LIKE A SHAW BROTHERS MOVIE
WE FOUND A HAPPY ENDING POST OUR TRAGEDIES
FUCK ALL THAT YOU HEARD, WE'RE NOT JUST SAD
    REFUGEES!
SO GRAB A DRINK, HOMIE, GRAB YO'SELF A GIRL
THIS SPOT'S OUR YARD, FREAK FLAGS UNFURL
MAD RESPECT'S GIVEN, THERE AIN'T NO FUCKIN' DOUBTS
WE THE KINGS HERE, SON, WE RUN THIS FUCKIN' HOUSE!

    *(**ALL** shout "yeah!" in agreement.)*
GOLDEN SKIN HOTTIES, THIN ASIAN BODIES,

NHAN.

THE KINDA HOT PARTY WHERE YOU WANT TO GET
    NAUGHTY
AND THERE AIN'T NO UGLY REDNECKS TRYNA RUIN THE
    MOOD
BY SAYIN' STUPID SHIT LIKE

ALL.

"SHOW US YOUR BOOBS!"

NHAN.

LISTEN UP, MY BROTHER, WHERE ELSE YOU WANNA BE?
INSIDE THESE FOUR WALLS, YOU A VIET BRUCE LEE
YOU'RE AN AIR FORCE CAPTAIN, HERE YOU'RE "THE
    DUDE"
ANYWHERE ELSE, YOU'RE JUST ANOTHER GOOK
SO WELCOME TO TEXAS – THIS PLACE WE CALL TEXAS
WE ALL UP IN TEXAS – LIKE A VIET NEXUS
LOOK AROUND, HOMIE, WHERE ELSE YOU WANNA GO?
FUCK ARKANSAS, THIS COULD BE YOUR HOME
SAIGON, TEXAS – ASIAN STRONG
A HOUSE UNDIVIDED, THIS IS WHERE YOU BELONG
SO STAND UP, HOMIE, THIS COULD BE YOUR LIFE
WELCOME TO TEXAS, AN ASIAN PARADISE

ALL.

HOUSTON!

> (**NHAN** *and* **QUANG** *at a club, slinging back drinks.*)

Look at this place, bro. Look at it. This is Vietnamese mecca!

> (**NHAN** *grabs a bowl of pho and feeds it to* **QUANG.***)*

I mean just taste this shit. Taste it. Put it in your mouth-hole.

> (**QUANG** *takes a bite.*)

QUANG. Daaaamn.

NHAN. And it's not just the food that's hot, we got clubs, we got community, we got jobs –

QUANG. You found a job here already?

NHAN. A bunch of old army grunts hooked me up with a gig selling stuff off the back of a truck.

QUANG. Off a truck? You're fencing shit?

NHAN. Am I selling discounted goods that may or may not have been illegally attained? Who am I to say?

QUANG. That's not the kind of job I'm looking for.

NHAN. Then we'll find you something better. Just look around, bro, this is basically Little Saigon. And you know what Saigon has? Ladies!

> (**NHAN** *points out a very attractive woman across the way.*)

QUANG. I got a wife.

NHAN. Yeah, a really pissed off wife who's probably right now working off her bad feelings on someone else's magic stick.

QUANG. Tong's not a cheater.

NHAN. Really? As I recall on Season One of *Vietgone,* she was in a committed relationship with some white dude named Bobby and you were still married when you both started playing "bumper crotch." Not only is she a cheater, you both are.

QUANG. Shit.

NHAN. But let me get your mind off your angry spouse and onto something more fun.

> (*A very drunk girl,* **SAN***, walks by, holding several drinks in hand.* **NHAN** *taps her on the shoulder.*)

NHAN. Hi there, can I introduce you to my friend Quang?

SAN. Hi Quang.

NHAN. Quang was the captain of my helicopter squadron. He's a hero who saved my life on multiple occasions. He also has an incredible body. I've seen it in the showers.

*(**SAN** hands her drinks to **NHAN**.)*

SAN. Do you mind bringing this to my friend over there? Thank you. Bye!

*(**NHAN** winks at **QUANG** as he walks away.)*

NHAN. Have fun!

SAN. So you fly helicopters? Is there a... Missus Helicopter?

*(**QUANG** pauses...but tells the truth.)*

QUANG. Uh...yeah.

SAN. You seem disappointed. Don't be. I'm married too.

QUANG. *(Relieved.)* Oh yeah?

SAN. His name was Bao. He was also a soldier boy. He didn't make it out though.

QUANG. He's still over there? Do you guys / write?

SAN. He's dead.

QUANG. Oh. Sorry.

SAN. That was seven years ago. I've dealt. But you're married – like currently married?

*(**QUANG** nods.)*

Too bad. Cause you look like you could be fun. Are you fun?

QUANG. I can be fun.

SAN. Too bad. I'm super fun too.

(She gives him a wink and leaves.)

*(**QUANG** stops her.)*

QUANG. We can still hang though, right? That's legal. Just hanging?

*(**SAN** thinks about it.)*

SAN. Yeah, we can hang.

(Cut to…)

*(**TONG** enters a restaurant. She's dressed nicely.)*

(She looks around, trying to find someone.)

(And then…)

BOBBY. Tong Thi Tran?

*(A smile crosses **TONG**'s face.)*

TONG. Bobby.

*(She turns and finds her ex-boyfriend **BOBBY** standing there.)*

(They don't know whether to hug or handshake.)

(They finally decide to awkwardly high-five.)

It's been a long time.

BOBBY. Yes. Big long time.

Sorry. Me Vietnamese is rust bucket. Long time since using it.

TONG. It's better than what I remembered.

How are you?

BOBBY. Me doing perfect!

TONG. That's great to hear. You look good. You've lost weight.

BOBBY. Me work out. Jazzercise!

(**BOBBY** *shows off some of his aerobics moves.*)

TONG. Cool?

BOBBY. Oh God, what me doing?

TONG. No, keep dancing. That's a totally a normal thing to do in a restaurant.

BOBBY. Okay.

(**BOBBY** *grabs* **TONG** *and spins her.*)

TONG. What are you doing?

BOBBY. What? Tong no dance no more?

(**TONG** *doesn't know how to answer this. She shakes it off.*)

TONG. We should get a table.

(*Cross cut with…*)

SAN. So is it true that pilots are all pussies?

QUANG. Who's the dumbass told you that?

SAN. My dead husband.

QUANG. Oh. Sorry.

SAN. He said all you fly-boys do is sit around in copters and get soft.

QUANG. I'm not soft.

SAN. Prove it.

QUANG. How do I prove –

*(***SAN*** rips open his shirt and touches his chest.)*

Okay now.

SAN. Nice.

Your wife is a very lucky woman. Tell me she appreciates this. 'Cause I would eat you up with a knife and fork.

QUANG. You're drunk.

SAN. YOU'RE drunk!

QUANG. She does appreciate me. But, ya know, we've been married for a minute. You know how it goes. Even this can get old.

SAN. Well then maybe you need something new.

(Focus shifts back to the restaurant.)

BOBBY. I super good. After Bobby leaving Tong –

TONG. I actually left you.

BOBBY. Bobby went into business for self, make Bobby his own boss, and now doing very big good.

TONG. What kind of business?

BOBBY. Number one salesmen in all of South Arkansas. I winning many awards. House full of awards.

TONG. That sounds great.

BOBBY. Me make good nice money.

TONG. Well, that's one of us. So...are you married now?

BOBBY. Bobby have girlfriend.

How is your guy man?

TONG. He's...great.

(Back to the club...)

SAN. Your wife still make you happy?

QUANG. *(Starts drunk crying.)* …

SAN. No?

QUANG. *(Through drunk tears.)* Of course she does, she's the best. Her smile is my most favorite thing in the world. I live for it.

SAN. *(Sympathetically drunk cries.)* Shit, that's sweet. I wish someone would say sweet shit like that about me.

QUANG. You have a nice smile, too.

(She slings back the last of her drink.)

SAN. I do?! It was nice meeting you, fly-boy. I should go home before I make any bad decisions.

QUANG. Do you want someone to walk you?

SAN. Nah, it's just around the corner. Goodnight, Quang.

QUANG. Goodnight, San.

SAN. I'll see you around.

(Restaurant…)

BOBBY. Bobby girlfriend is crazy pretty. No, that wrong word. Crazy beautiful. That's it. She is crazy crazy CRAZY girl. Very CRAZY.

TONG. I think you're emphasizing the wrong word.

BOBBY. Me happy. That's what Tong needing to know. Bobby is very happy.

(Back at the Club…)

*(**SAN** reenters the bar.)*

QUANG. Hey. What are you doing back here?

SAN. I accidentally left something.

QUANG. What's that?

SAN. You! You're coming home with me, okay?!

> (**SAN** *drags* **QUANG** *out of the bar by the collar.*)

> *(Restaurant...)*

TONG. I'm not happy.

BOBBY. What?

TONG. I'm not. I'm broke, Quang and I are technically not even married anymore, and now I'm about to lose my job.

BOBBY. You're not married?

TONG. I thought life here would be easier than this. That if I just worked really hard here, "I could be anything I wanted to be." That's what this place promises, right? Vietnam sucks, but at least people there saw me as a person and not just some "immigrant."

I'm sorry, I don't mean to throw all that on you. It's just that –

BOBBY. *Me have no girlfriend!*

TONG. What?

BOBBY. Bobby crazy girlfriend not real. Me only wanting to making you to feeling jealous.

TONG. Well, I don't feel great. Does that count?

BOBBY. No. Bobby not want Tong to feeling bad. Bobby never wanting Tong to feeling bad. Bobby only wanting Tong to feeling safe. Protected. Taken care of.

> *(Their eyes lock. They go in for a kiss, but* **TONG** *accidentally knocks over a glass of water.)*

TONG. I'm sorry. I shouldn't be here. This was all – I should go home. Thank you so much for listening. It was good seeing you again.

BOBBY. Goodbye, Tong.

TONG. Goodbye, Bobby.

(She hugs him and leaves.)

7.

*(Lights up on **LITTLE MAN** playing with his Spider-Man action figure in the front lawn.)*

*(**HUONG** approaches with a guitar case.)*

HUONG. Hey!

LITTLE MAN. Grandma! Why do you have a guitar?

HUONG. You're having problems at school, right?

(She drops the case.)

LITTLE MAN. Yeah. No one talks to me. And the ones that do aren't so nice.

HUONG. Well, I'm here to fix all that.

LITTLE MAN. Are you going to teach me?

HUONG. Sure am.

LITTLE MAN. Like music?

HUONG. Better.

LITTLE MAN. Better?

*(**HUONG** clicks open the guitar case...)*

HUONG. I'm gonna teach you the only thing you really need to know in life – how to *kick ass.*

(...And pulls out a bokken.)

LITTLE MAN. Is that a sword?

HUONG. It's a *bokken.* A wooden Japanese training blade. But you're not quite ready for this.

*(She puts the sword down and sits beside **LITTLE MAN**. She puts up her hands.)*

Okay. Now look at my hands.

(She slaps him.)

LITTLE MAN. Ow!

HUONG. No, block it.

(She slaps him again.)

LITTLE MAN. Ow!

HUONG. No, with your arm, not your face.

(She slaps him again.)

LITTLE MAN. Ow.

HUONG. Oh my god, this is going to take forever.

LITTLE MAN. I'm sorry.

HUONG. NO. Don't be sorry. Be ready. Because, my little Pinocchio, I'm turning you into a real life badass.

(A song in the style of "Eye Of The Tiger" begins to play.)*

(A montage sequence.)

*(– **HUONG** bows to **LITTLE MAN**. **LITTLE MAN** begins to bow as well, but **HUONG** slaps his head. She indicates that he should always keeps his eyes on his opponents.)*

---

* A license to produce *Poor Yella Rednecks* does not include a performance license for "Eye of the Tiger" by Survivor. The publisher and author suggest that the licensee contact ASCAP or BMI to ascertain the music publisher and contact such music publisher to license or acquire permission for performance of the song. If a license or permission is unattainable for "Eye of the Tiger," the licensee may not use the song in *Poor Yella Rednecks* but should create an original composition in a similar style or use a similar song in the public domain. For further information, please see the Music and Third-Party Materials Use Note on page iii.

*(– **HUONG** shows him a crescent kick. He tries and falls on his ass.)*

*(– **HUONG** gets him to run laps by making him chase a Spider-Man action figure dangling off a fishing pole. As **LITTLE MAN** runs after it, he leaps over a dog, a mailbox, and finally…slams directly into a tree.)*

*(– **HUONG** commands **LITTLE MAN** back onto his feet. She shows him the crescent kick again, but he again fails to do it and lands on his butt.)*

(– She goes to help him up, but he suddenly blocks her hand.)

(– Impressed, she gets into a fight stance, as does he. She attacks him and he's able to avoid/block all the hits.)

(– With approval, she commands him to do a pushup. And then a single arm pushup. And then a single arm pushup with a boulder on his back.)

(– Impressed with how strong he's become, she makes him karate chop a wooden board in half – which he does with ease. To up the ante, she brings in a cinder block. He tries to karate chop it twice but fails on both occassions. Finally, he headbutts it in half. He celebrates the win, but then holds his head in pain.)

*(– Realizing he's ready for the final challenge. **HUONG** grabs the bokken and takes a swing at his feet, **LITTLE MAN** leaps out of the way as – in slow mo – she goes to chop him in half. He however catches the blade with his palms*

and finally executes the crescent kick to knock the blade away.)

(– But before he can celebrate, two trucks drive towards him and he leaps into a split, holding them off [Jean Claude Van Damme style] before finally kicking them away.)

(– It ends with **HUONG** *and* **LITTLE MAN** *bowing to each other.)*

(– She grabs him and hugs him, so proud of what he's accomplished. They exit with him riding on her shoulder like he's won the Superbowl.)

8.

*(Back at home, **QUANG** is filling out job applications when **TONG** comes in.)*

TONG. *(Visibly upset.)* Hey there. So how was your day today?

QUANG. Is there something / wrong –

TONG. Mine was lovely, but a little weird. How was it weird exactly? Oh I don't know, just kinda weird in the sense that it was pretty fucking weird, like the kinda weird that comes when you think a thing is a thing but that thing turns out to be bullshit. I had one of those days.

*(No response from **QUANG**.)*

Oh, you have that look. That "I'm so fucking busted" look, but "not exactly sure what specifically I got busted on." Wanna venture a guess?

*(No response from **QUANG**.)*

You should probably say something before I stab you.

QUANG. You found out about the girl.

TONG. …

QUANG. It is about the girl, right?

TONG. Which girl would that be?

QUANG. There was only the one.

TONG. Are you sure there's not two?

QUANG. I'm pretty sure there's not two.

TONG. And I'm pretty sure I wasn't talking about any girl. I had no idea you were fucking anyone else. But thanks for throwing that in there as well.

QUANG. What's this about?

TONG. Our Little Man is getting shit at school. The kids there are all dumb as fuck and the teachers are useless. I tried to talk to them about it and they just stare at me with those dumbass smiles like I'm too foreign to understand when I'm being talked down to. Thought it'd be easier to put the little man somewhere where I can have more of a direct say about how he's being taught as in… I wanna pay someone to do their fucking job so if and when they fuck up, I can just fire their useless American ass.

QUANG. So this is about school?

TONG. This is about the FIVE THOUSAND DOLLARS that was in our bank account and now isn't.

QUANG. I can explain. I was going to put it back.

TONG. Is this for some girl you're fucking? 'Cause I assumed it was missing because you sent it to Vietnam. To your wife.

QUANG. …

TONG. So asshole, which bitch is the one fucking me right now?

QUANG. It's for my kids.

TONG. Your kids? Right.

QUANG. I'm not lying – it's for them. It kills me that they're over there thinking that I abandoned them. I want them to know their dad still cares. I'm never going to see them or hold them again so I thought a little help might ease their pain.

> (**TONG** *considers his words.*)

TONG. You know that's great. That's really fucking great. 'Cause now I'm the big fucking asshole for not having sympathy for the fact that you took the only money we had – money that I made – and gave it away to "your kids." But what about mine? Ours? Do I need to remind you that you have a son here too? And I don't know if you noticed between your affairs and your guilt and your need to run away to Texas, but that son isn't doing so well right now. He has no friends, his teachers can't talk to him, and he spends all day with my crazy ass mother while I work my ass off. So it's great that you're telling yourself that you're doing what you're doing out of love and nobility, but a lie is still a lie – regardless of which wife you're telling it to.

QUANG. Tong.

[MUSIC NO. 05 – LET ME REINTRODUCE MYSELF (REPRISE)]

(A beat drops.)

TONG. *(Rapped.)*
LEMME REINTRODUCE MYSELF
I'M THAT GIRL YOU SWORE YOU'D ALWAYS PROTECT
I GUESS I GUESS THOSE WORDS WERE JUST WORDS TO
    YOU
I GUESS THE ONLY ONE YOU CARE ABOUT HERE IS YOU
I SHOULDA KNOWN – IT WAS HOT AIR YOU WERE BLOWIN'
I SHOULDA SEEN – PAST ALL THEM LINES YOU WERE
    THROWIN'
WHEN SHIT GETS TOUGH – YO, YOUR CHARACTER IS
    SHOWIN'
YOU'LL RUN AWAY FASTER THAN JESSE OWENS
YA PROMISED ME THE WORLD – TO ALWAYS BE MINE
BUT I'M A FUCKING IDIOT FOR BUYING YOUR LINES
BUT THAT'S OKAY, BABY, I DON'T NEED A "RIDE OR DIE"
I'M JUST GLAD I CAUGHT YOU NOW IN THE MIDDLE OF
    YOUR LIES
AND I GOTTA SAY, BABY, I'M SO MUCH BETTER THAN YOU
'CAUSE WHAT I GOT HERE IS SO MUCH SMARTER THAN YOU
AND IN THE BEDROOM, GONNA HAVE MORE FUN THAN YOU

BUT MOST IMPORTANTLY IMMA BE RICHER THAN YOU
NOW THAT I FOUND OUT, MY HEART'S UP AND CLOSED
DON'T GIVE A SHIT 'BOUT NO HOES YOU BONED
I'M DONE – WE THROUGH – TURN AROUND – GO
IMMA SAY IT AGAIN, GET THE FUCK OUT MY HOME
AND WHEN HE ASKS ABOUT YOU – OUR BEAUTIFUL SON
DON'T THINK IMMA HOLD BACK MY MOTHERFUCKIN'
    TONGUE
IMMA TELL HIM THE TRUTH – HON, YOUR DAD'S A
    FUCKING BUM
WHEN SHIT GETS HAIRY, HE UP AND RUNS
SO FUCK YOU, BABY, FUCK ALL THAT YOU SAID
FUCK EV'RY SINGLE PROMISE YOU MADE SINCE WE MET
FUCK YOU, BABY, FUCK ALL YOUR LIES
FUCK EVERY DOLLAR YOU STOLE AND GAVE TO YOUR
    WIFE

    (**QUANG** *leaves.*)

FUCK YOU, BABY, FUCK EVERYTHING YOU'LL BE
FUCK THIS GODDAMN PLACE FROM SEA TO SHINING SEA
FUCK YOU, BABY, FUCK THIS MOMENT RIGHT NOW
CUZ I'M DONE WITH YOUR SHIT. FUCK OFF. I'M OUT.

    (**TONG** *stands strong.*)

    (*She collapses.*)

    (*Blackout.*)

End of Act One

ACT TWO

1.

(A dark stage…)

STAN LEE. *(Voice-over.)* Greetings, true believers. Now let's take a sneak peek into the life of our mighty but miniature hero while he works on training up his mental superpowers of imagination.

> *(Lights up on **LITTLE MAN**, playing with his action figure, singing a superhero theme song.*)*
>
> *(Out from the edges of the stage, enter two bullies, **TOMMY** and **CHRIS**.)*

TOMMY. Yee-haw yee-haw it's the ching chong kid yee-haw.

LITTLE MAN. Leave me alone.

CHRIS. Yee-haw yee-haw go back to China yee-haw.

TOMMY. Or we'll send you back there ourselves yee-haw.

LITTLE MAN. No. I'm going to sit here and play with my Spider-Man. You can't stop me.

TOMMY. Yee-haw yee-haw I don't see how you're gonna do that yee-haw.

---

* A license to produce *Poor Yella Rednecks* does not include a license to publicly display any branded logos or trademarked images, or perform any third-party or copyrighted music. Licensees must acquire rights for any logos and/or images or create their own.

(**CHRIS** *snatches Little Man's action figure out of his hands.*)

CHRIS. Especially since this is now our Spider-Man.

LITTLE MAN. Give it back.

TOMMY. What are you gonna do about it yee-haw?

STAN LEE. *(Voice-over.)* And that's when our little mighty hero remembered a very important lesson from his grandmother.

(Spotlight on **HUONG.***)*

HUONG. If they mess with you... Kick. Their. Asses.

LITTLE MAN. You made me mad. You shouldn't have made me mad. I'm going to kick your ass now.

(A badass remix of a '60s superhero theme song kicks in.)*

(Fight/movement sequence: A huge theatrical fight ensues where **LITTLE MAN** *beats the shit out of the* **BULLIES** *"Spidey-style.")*

(Note: You may want to use two different **LITTLE MAN** *puppets here to get the most out of this fun action sequence...also to maybe do the whole "two Spider-Men pointing at eachother meme" which is fun.)*

(At the end, **LITTLE MAN** *stands over the fallen* **BULLIES.***)*

TONG. *(Steps onstage.)* Qui Truong Nguyen, WHAT THE FUCK??? Get your ass home right now!!

---

* A license to produce *Poor Yella Rednecks* does not include a performance license for any third-party or copyrighted music. Licensees should create an original composition or use music in the public domain. For further information, please see the Music and Third-Party Materials Use Note on page iii.

2.

*(Back at home, **TONG** stares **LITTLE MAN** down. **LITTLE MAN** avoids her gaze.)*

TONG. Now repeat:

*(**HUONG** watches from afar.)*

"I will not Hulk Hogan the Honky Tonk Piggly Wigglies at Saved by the Bell."

LITTLE MAN. What?

TONG. "I will not Hulk Hogan the Honky Tonk Piggly Wigglies at Saved by the Bell." Say it.

LITTLE MAN. It doesn't make sense.

TONG. "I will not Hulk Hogan –"

LITTLE MAN. Mommy! Stop! I don't understand!

TONG. You're the one who decided to get into a fight. Now repeat. In English. "I will not Hulk Hogan –"

LITTLE MAN. I don't like English!

TONG. "– The Honky Tonk Piggly Wigglies –"

LITTLE MAN. STOP IT!

TONG. "– at Saved by the Bell!"

LITTLE MAN. Stop stop stop stop.

HUONG. That's enough. She's asking you to repeat "I will not beat up the stupid ass white kids at school anymore."

TONG. Mom, stay out of this.

HUONG. He's a little kid. He was getting picked on. He has the right to defend himself.

TONG. Mom, they're threatening to expel him from school. I need you to be on my side right now.

HUONG. I'm always on your side. But right now it's not your side that needs defending.

TONG. He can't just punch kids.

HUONG. So what he's supposed to do? Not punch bullies because "punching people is bad?"

TONG. YES!

HUONG. Well, that's stupid.

LITTLE MAN. Stop yelling.

TONG. He's getting picked on because he can't speak English, Mom. That's something I asked you to help him with, but instead –

HUONG. Do not throw this on me! This has nothing to do with English. They're shitty ass crap people, that's why they mess with him.

LITTLE MAN. Mom.

TONG. They're just kids.

HUONG. They're dicks!

LITTLE MAN. *(Yells out.)* I will not Hulk Hogan the Honky Tonk Piggly Wigglies at Saved by the Bell!

TONG. What was that?

LITTLE MAN. I won't Hulk Hogan again, Mommy. Or Bruce Lee. Or Chuck Norris. I promise.

Just stop yelling at each other, okay? Please.

TONG. Ross and Rachel, Chandler. Ross and Rachel.

*(She kisses **LITTLE MAN** on the forehead.)*

HUONG. Hey. You need to get to work.

TONG. Right. Okay. I'm going to be late tonight. I'm pulling a double. Gotta make what I can before the diner closes. And Mom, try not to talk to him too much. It's not good for him.

HUONG. Gotcha. Don't talk. You can trust me.

(**TONG** *leaves.*)

Do you wanna go take a walk down to the corner store? Grandma needs a beer. Come on, I'll buy you an Icee.

(*Exit language:*)

LITTLE MAN. What's happening?

HUONG. Your mom's losing her shit, that's what's happening. But don't worry! This is nothing compared to how badly she lost it at her little brother, Uncle Khue, when he told her he was staying in Vietnam because of love. But he has two kids now, you know? So who's the real dummy?

3.

(**TONG** *is closing up the diner.*)

(**QUANG** *enters with flowers.*)

QUANG. Hey... I drove by and saw you were closing up – I thought I'd come in and tell you, I talked to a lawyer – Thu and I are done, which means you and I –

TONG. No.

QUANG. Can we not just talk about this?

TONG. I'm not ready.

QUANG. Why does this have to be such a big deal?

TONG. I just said I'm not ready.

QUANG. I just want to know what I can do to make things better.

TONG. Get a time machine, go back, and not meet me.

QUANG. You don't mean that.

TONG. Right now, I kinda do.

QUANG. Let me fix this.

TONG. I don't want you to fix this.

QUANG. Why can't I at least try to make this better?

TONG. Because I'm tired of depending on other people to get my shit done.

QUANG. What does that mean?

TONG. It means...you go take care of Thu and your kids over there. I'll take care of me, my mom, and our Little Man here. I got this now.

QUANG. You can't.

TONG. I can. And I am.

[MUSIC NO. 06 – POOR YELLA REDNECKS]

(A beat drops.)

(Rapped.)

BETTER CHECK WHAT I'M SAYING
CUZ YOUR SHORTY AIN'T PLAYING
GOT MY OWN PLANS NOW, BABY,
AND MY TIME – I'M DONE WASTING
FUCK COMPLAINING (THAT AIN'T ME)
YOU FRUSTRATED? (YO HATE ME)
PEEPING AT YOUR EX, SEEING THAT SHE'S SLAYING DAILY
    (YAY ME)
I'M SO FUCKING CLEVER
FUCKING FLY FOREVER
SIT BACK AND WATCH ME WIN BIG AT ALL I ENDEAVOR
    (CLEVER)
NO MATTER WHAT THE SITCH THO,
I'LL NEVER QUIT THO
THIS PLACE CAN GIVE ME SHIT BUT I DON'T GIVE A SHIT
    THO
CUZ I'M MORE THAN JUST PRETTY,
MY BRAIN IS DAMN WITTY
GIMME ONE HOT SECOND – IMMA RUN THIS CITY
YO, SAY THAT I SHOULDN'T – I'M MY OWN WOMAN
I'M STRONGER THAN ANY MAN AND TWICE AS GOOD
    LOOKIN'

(Lights up on **HUONG** *with* **LITTLE MAN** *as* **TONG** *returns home.)*

HUONG. *(To* **LITTLE MAN**.*)*

EVEN IF THEY MAD AT YOU, YOU GOTTA BE TRUE TO YOU
EV'RY SCAR YOU WEAR, YOU SHOW THE SHIT THAT YOU
    WENT THROUGH

HUONG.
> YA GOTTA STAND STRONG, BE STRONG, HEADSTRONG, YA AIN'T WRONG
> SO COME ON LISTEN CLOSE, THIS HERE'S OUR FIGHT SONG

TONG. *(To* **LITTLE MAN.***)*
> I'M A POOR YELLA REDNECK
> I DEMAND RESPECT
> AIN'T GOT ALOTTA MONEY
> BUT I'M STILL DAMN PERFECT
> HAVE PRIDE IN US, SON
> LISTEN TO MY REASON
> YOUR MOMMA'S WORKING HARD WHILE THE REST OF THEM ARE SLEEPING

> *(To the audience.)*

> FUCK A BUNCHA PRETENSE
> LEMME START A NEW SENTENCE
> GOT NO TIME TO DEAL WITH ANY OF THIS FOOLISH WHACKASS NONSENSE
> I REFUSE TO BE HOPELESS,
> MY EYES – STRAIGHT FOCUSED
> I AIM AT MY HIGHEST EVEN WHEN I'M AT MY LOWEST (KNOW THIS)
> WHILE THE REST ARE DREAMING
> MY MIND IS ALWAYS SCHEMING (MEANING)
> THROW THAT GLASS AROUND ME, IMMA SMASH THROUGH THAT CEILING (REACHING)

> I'M A JUNGLE ASIAN – I'M GOOD AT EQUATIONS
> AND KICKING PEOPLE'S ASS, WHILE INSIDE I'M STILL RAGING
> I'M CLIMBING THESE LADDERS,
> ADAPTING THROUGH DISASTERS
> NO MONEY IN MY POCKET BUT I'M RICH WHERE IT MATTERS
> WON'T STOP TILL WE'VE WON, SON

SWINGING FOR THAT HOME RUN
LIKE THE SONG SAYS,

COMPANY.
"IMMIGRANTS: WE GET THE JOB DONE!"
DON'T GOT ALOTTA OPTIONS
DON'T GOT ALOTTA CASH
WE GOT ALOTTA PROBLEMS

COMPANY.
YOU CAN KISS OUR ASS!

TONG.
WE POOR AS FUCK
YELLA AS WELL
NOTHING STOPPING US
WE MAD AS –

COMPANY. – Hell!

(Rapped.)

POOR YELLA REDNECKS
WE DEMAND RESPECT
AIN'T GOT ALOTTA MONEY
BUT WE'RE STILL DAMN PERFECT
ROSE UP, SON
LISTEN TO OUR REASON
WE'RE CLIMBING MOUNTAINS WHILE THE REST OF THEM
    ARE SLEEPING
POOR YELLA REDNECKS
WE DEMAND RESPECT
AIN'T GOT ALOTTA MONEY
BUT WE'RE STILL DAMN PERFECT
HAVE PRIDE, SON
LISTEN TO OUR REASON

TONG.
YOUR MOMMA'S WORKING HARD WHILE THE REST OF
    THEM ARE SLEEPING.

4.

*(**TONG** brings **BOBBY** into her home for the first time. She looks around as they quietly enter.)*

TONG. *(Quietly.)* Hey Mom, you asleep?

BOBBY. So this place you live?

(Trying but failing to be nice.) It...nice.

TONG. Don't lie.

BOBBY. It not nice.

TONG. It's a roof. It's safe. I've had worse.

*(**HUONG** runs in with a knife.)*

BOBBY. Oh God!

TONG. Mom, put the knife down.

HUONG. Ugh, this dummy again?

TONG. He's a friend. He's visiting.

HUONG. It's pretty late for a friend to be over.

TONG. Okay, he might be more than a friend.

HUONG. God. Really? Him? There's so many other white guys out there. Can't you pick one that's not a dummy.

TONG. He's a good guy. I didn't give him a fair shake before.

HUONG. What's he do for a living?

TONG. I don't want to be with him for his money.

HUONG. So he's that loaded now?

TONG. No. I don't know. We're just hanging out.

HUONG. Fine. Whatever. Just...don't make too much noise out here. And put down a towel, we have to sit on that couch.

TONG. MOM!

HUONG. Whatever. You know it's true.

(**HUONG** *leaves.*)

BOBBY. She no change at all. Same look in face. Very pretty...and angry. Always so angry.

TONG. That's my mom.

BOBBY. Bobby wanting to say – seeing Tong again is like... being in place where dead people go who believe in Jesus.

You still making me feel princess awesome happy.

TONG. I do?

(**TONG** *stares at him.*)

BOBBY. Wanting to see what is on TV?

TONG. Kiss me.

BOBBY. Okay.

(**BOBBY** *tries to find his fortitude. He leans in and...starts crying.*)

TONG. Um, what's happening?

BOBBY. (*Sobbing.*) Sorry. Me am so sorry. For big long time, Bobby dream-think about Tong. But me never think Tong will ever be kissing Bobby again. Bobby just so over-full with happy awesome.

TONG. That's so sweet. But maybe this time – can you kiss me again but without the crying?

(**BOBBY** *nods, kisses* **TONG.** *It's super lame.*)

BOBBY. Is this too fast too furious?

TONG. No.

BOBBY. You want slow down?

TONG. Just relax. Okay?

> *(She sits him down, gets behind him and massages his shoulders – he giggles.)*

BOBBY. Sorry.

> *(She goes to massage him some more, but he wigs out and falls on the floor to get away.)*

(Stands up.) Sorry. Neck is Tickle-me-Elmo. I very – not expecting that.

> **(TONG** *stops.)*

TONG. You know what? It's cool. Maybe we're rushing.

BOBBY. Yes. Very fast. Very rushing.

TONG. I'll just...do you wanna watch TV?

> **(BOBBY** *nods.)*

> **(TONG** *looks for the TV remote.)*

BOBBY. Can Bobby asking Tong question?

TONG. Sure. What is it?

BOBBY. Why Quang?

TONG. Why'd I leave him? Let me count the ways. He's still in love with his ex-wife, he's irresponsible, and financially, a total fucking disaster. I think that about sums it up.

Speaking of...what do you do for a living?

BOBBY. I sell.

TONG. You're in marketing?

BOBBY. Tupperware.

TONG. Tupper...?

BOBBY. Plastic containers. Keep all food dry and fresh. Do you want some? I can sell special small price to Tong.

TONG. I'm good.

BOBBY. But that not what me asking. Me asking why Quang, not Bobby?

TONG. Oh. THAT. I don't know.

(*Thinks about* **QUANG**.)

I was dumb. I think I was lost. He was lost too. It just made sense to be lost together.

(*Re-directs.*) But I'm done being lost. I'm ready for direction now.

BOBBY. And Bobby is that direction?

TONG. You could be.

(*Playfully.*) If you weren't so fucking ticklish...

(**BOBBY** *boldly walks up to* **TONG**.)

(*Impressed.*) Okay now, what is this?

(*He leans in and they bonk heads.*)

Ow!

BOBBY. OH GOD. Sorry. I'm so sorry.

TONG. This isn't going to work.

BOBBY. I'll go home now.

TONG. (*Stops him.*) That's not what I mean. I mean I don't think you should be the one leading this dance.

(**TONG** *straddles him.*)

Let me.

(*They start making out.*)

5.

(At a fast food restaurant.)

QUANG. So you've probably been wondering where I've been, right?

LITTLE MAN. Nope.

QUANG. You haven't?

LITTLE MAN. Have you been somewhere, Daddy?

QUANG. Well, I haven't been home.

LITTLE MAN. I know. Mom told me.

QUANG. She did? And you're okay with it?

LITTLE MAN. Of course, Daddy. Why wouldn't I be?

QUANG. Oh, okay. I thought you'd be upset.

(LITTLE MAN *laughs at his* **DAD.)**

LITTLE MAN. Why would I be upset? Mom told me you got a new job that made you wake up early in the morning and come home late at night.

QUANG. Oh. So you think –

LITTLE MAN. Is that not what happened?

QUANG. *(Redirects.)* Um...it's... I got you something.

(QUANG *pulls out something wrapped in newspaper.)*

LITTLE MAN. What's this?

QUANG. It's a present. For you, buddy. Open it.

(LITTLE MAN *tears into it. Inside he finds...)*

LITTLE MAN. Holy fucking shit!!

QUANG. Qui, language.

LITTLE MAN. Yes, Dad. I promise never to swear in public ever again... But it's an Atari!!

(**LITTLE MAN** *starts crying happy tears.*)

QUANG. I got it from Jimmy. His son melted a crayon on it and broke one of the controllers, but otherwise it works pretty good.

LITTLE MAN. Why'd you get me this?

QUANG. You're a good kid. You deserve something nice. Especially right now.

LITTLE MAN. What's happening right now?

QUANG. It's...um...

(**QUANG** *wants to lie...but can't.*)

Well, bud, the thing is...your mom and I both love you so much...so very much, but...

(*Confesses.*) We're not doing so well.

LITTLE MAN. (*Freaks out.*) You're dying???

QUANG. What? No, I'm not dying.

LITTLE MAN. (*Even more freaked out.*) *Mommy's dying???*

QUANG. No.

LITTLE MAN. But you said you're not doing well –

QUANG. Emotionally. Emotionally we're not doing well, but physically we're fine. Completely healthy.

LITTLE MAN. So no one's dying?

QUANG. Not anytime soon.

LITTLE MAN. Then what do you mean you and Mom aren't doing well?

QUANG. I mean… I don't have a job that I have to "wake up early and come home late for." I'm not home because I moved out of the house.

LITTLE MAN. Why?

QUANG. It's grown up stuff, bud. But none of it's your fault. I just need you to understand that.

LITTLE MAN. Are you and Mommy not married anymore?

QUANG. I don't know what we are.

LITTLE MAN. Do you not love her?

QUANG. Of course I do, bud. I love Mommy with all my heart. Every bit of it. She's still my everything. But Daddy messed up. He messed up real bad, so…if you want to be mad at someone for what's happening right now, if you need someone to blame – blame me, okay? It's not your mommy's fault. It's mine. Daddy messed up everything.

LITTLE MAN. Daddy, don't be sad.

When I mess up stuff, Grandma just tells me to clean it up. Just clean it up. Okay?

QUANG. I'll try.

(They hug.)

6.

*(Back at home, **TONG** sits at the kitchen table with a Vietnamese/English dictionary and a set of forms in front of her.)*

*(**HUONG** enters, watches her **DAUGHTER** as...)*

*(**TONG** keeps trying to decipher something, but it's not clear. She finally crumples it up and tosses it.)*

TONG. Fuck!

HUONG. You missed.

TONG. Go away, Mom.

HUONG. *(Picks up the form.)* What is this?

TONG. Just leave it.

HUONG. *(Drops it in the trashcan.)* I'm just trying to help.

TONG. You being helpful? That'd be a first.

HUONG. Hey. I watch Little Man. That's help. REAL help. So you can work.

TONG. Well. It's three p.m. on a Thursday. Clearly work isn't a problem.

HUONG. Then shouldn't you be out there looking for a job instead of in here curled up like an angry armadillo?

TONG. That's what I'm doing, Mom. That's what these are.

McDonald's. Safeway. Tiger Harry's. I've literally been to every store in the square.

HUONG. Then what's the / problem?

TONG. I can't fucking read any of it. So do you want to help? How's your mastery of English these days?

HUONG. Can you ask your boyfriend for help?

TONG. His English is fine, but his Vietnamese sucks.

HUONG. I didn't mean with the job application. I mean... he could give you money.

TONG. Mom. No. I'm not – NO.

HUONG. You know he'd do it. Look at you. You're an Asian nine, he's a non-Asian four at best. Fucking him is already a charity case, you might as well get some cash out of it too.

TONG. That's fucking gross.

HUONG. I just –

TONG. Don't, Mom. Just don't.

And why are you lingering over me anyways?

HUONG. We're out of a few things. I can go pick them up, I just need some cash.

> (**TONG** *snags the grocery list out of her* **MOTHER***'s hands.*)

TONG. No. I'll do it. I need a break from this shit anyways. Besides I don't need to get a call about you yelling at people at the store again. Just stay here and watch Little Man, okay? I'll be back home in a minute.

> (**TONG** *exits as* **HUONG** *watches on...*)

HUONG. Mu. I really fucked this up.

> (*Cut to...*)

STAN LEE VOICE-OVER. (*Over superhero theme music.**) And now, true believers, let's turn our focus to our

---

* A license to produce *Poor Yella Rednecks* does not include a performance license for any third-party or copyrighted music. Licensees should create an original composition or use music in the public domain. For further information, please see the Music and Third-Party Materials Use Note on page iii.

impoverished protagonist as she faces her next great challenge – procuring supplies while penniless. Excelsior!

> *(Grocery store music.* **TONG** *pushes a grocery cart through a Safeway. She adds the prices of the items in her cart...)*

TONG. Five and three is eight. Eight plus another four is twelve. Twelve plus fifteen is... FUCK!

> *(***TONG*** *opens her purse and sees she only has seven dollars on her.)*
>
> *(She looks around to see if anyone's looking her direction.)*
>
> *(She grabs a couple of the items in the cart and slides them into her purse.)*
>
> *(A* **GROCERY BOY** *sees her stealing the food. Sneaks up, grabs her arm.)*

GROCERY BOY. CLEANUP ON AISLE FOUR!!!!

> *(She pushes him away.)*

TONG. Stay away from me!

GROCERY BOY. Drop it like it's hot!

TONG. You don't understand, I need this.

> *(A* **SECOND GROCER** *approaches.)*

SECOND GROCER. *(Sees what's happening.)* Fuck a duck, Starsky and Hutch!

---

* A license to produce *Poor Yella Rednecks* does not include a performance license for any third-party or copyrighted music. Licensees should create an original composition or use music in the public domain. For further information, please see the Music and Third-Party Materials Use Note on page iii.

SECOND GROCER. *(Suddenly super aggro.)* By the power of Greyskull. HE-MAN!

TONG. It's just a little food.

GROCERY BOY. Arthur Fonzarelli, Egg roll. Arthur Fonzarelli.

> *(**TONG** sees she's cornered.)*

> *(She contemplates giving the **GROCERS** what's in her purse, but then decides...)*

TONG. You know what? Since we're already here...

> *(She grabs more things out of her shopping cart and drops them into her purse.)*

You wanna go, assholes? Then let's go.

> *(She steps back into a fight stance.)*

> *(The two **GROCERS** look at each other and know what they gotta do.)*

BOTH GROCERS. CLOOOCK-WORK OOOR-ANGE!!!!

> *(The two **GROCERS** move to attack when...)*

> *(Ding! Everything freezes as **PLAYWRIGHT** enters.)*

PLAYWRIGHT. According to the real life accounts of Tong Nguyen, what happens next is all completely true.

> *(Unfreeze. Music like Dolly Parton's "9 to 5" pumps in as...*)*

---

* A license to produce *Poor Yella Rednecks* does not include a performance license for "9 to 5" by Dolly Parton. The publisher and author suggest that the licensee contact ASCAP or BMI to ascertain the music publisher and contact such music publisher to license or acquire permission for performance of the song. If a license or permission is unattainable for "9 to 5," the licensee may not use the song in *Poor Yella Rednecks* but should create an original composition in a similar style or use a similar song in the public domain. For further information, please see the Music and Third-Party Materials Use Note on page iii.

*(Fight/movement sequence: In the greatest fight sequence ever to be seen on a live stage, **TONG** fights the **GROCERS**, Bruce Lee-style. It begins with just unarmed hand-to-hand combat and escalates to katanas and nunchucks. It's all over-the-top ultra-violent [though never murderous]. It ends when she knocks them out.)*

*(She goes to exit and finds a **COP** staring her down, with a stun-gun in hand.)*

COP. Yee-haw it's over yee-haw. Drop the purse, yee-haw.

*(**TONG** raises her arms.)*

TONG. Fuck.

7.

> (**QUANG** *is at the police station, addressing an unseen cop.*)

QUANG. What's that, Officer? She did what?

No, I'm not technically her...

Do you even understand what I'm saying?

Whatever. Yeah, I'll take her.

I said I WILL. TAKE. HER.

> *(Cut to...)*

> (**QUANG** *now sits on the back of a truck bed with* **TONG**.)

> *(A pizza box and fast food bags sit between them.)*

> *(They're giggling [clearly stoned] as they eat fast food.)*

> (**TONG** *has an entire burger sandwiched between two slices of pizza.*)

TONG. Oh my God. Look at this shit. I call it a pizzaburger! Try it! Stick it in your mouth. Just the tip just the tip.

> *(She shoves the pizza sandwich in* **QUANG**'s *face.)*

Do it.

QUANG. *(Takes a bite.)* Goddamn.

TONG. This woulda been so good at the diner.

They loved them some new shit. I miss that place.

Those customers were the closest thing I had to friends here.

(Through laughter.) Which is sad. Super sad.

(Sudden tears.)

Everything is sad.

(An epiphany.) Except for this genius food invention I just made. You ain't sad, you fucking amazing.

QUANG. You're stoned.

TONG. No, YOU'RE stoned.

QUANG. I can't believe I'm actually smoking pot with you again.

TONG. Why are you so surprised? Is that because you think I'm super straight-laced now that I'm dating a white guy?

QUANG. I just thought moments like these were behind us.

TONG. Yeah. Well. Me too.

(Contemplative moment of quiet.)

Thanks for bailing me out.

QUANG. I can't believe you got arrested. Badass.

TONG. I'm glad you appreciate my violent proclivities. How are you doing?

QUANG. I'm okay. Started working at a cable factory. Cutting cable. It's almost twenty hours a week.

TONG. That's good.

QUANG. And you?

TONG. Oh you know how it is. It's super easy getting work here when your English is for shit.

QUANG. Right.

TONG. But one of the old customers at the diner, Mister Sinclair, offered me a job at his paper bag company.

QUANG. That's good.

TONG. Except it's in Crossett. I'd never be home, I'd never see Little Man. And the best part – it pays even less than what I made at the diner.

QUANG. So not the dream job?

TONG. Almost. But not quite.

QUANG. So...how is, um, Bobby?

TONG. He's okay. Steady. Predictable. Stable.

QUANG. That sounds...sexy.

TONG. Fuck off.

QUANG. What? Nothing sounds sexier than "stable."

TONG. When you haven't had it, like ever, it's sexier than you think it is. Don't knock it.

QUANG. Sorry, I don't mean to talk shit. It's just an instinct.

TONG. I get it.

QUANG. What's he do for a living?

TONG. What?

QUANG. What does he do to be, ya know, "stable?"

TONG. He sells stuff. All sorts of stuff.

QUANG. Yo, is Bobby a drug dealer?

TONG. NO! It's not important. Let's just drop it, okay?

(*She can't drop it.*)

Tupperware! He sells fucking Tupperware.

It's shit housewives buy. He's a fucking Avon lady.

QUANG. Oh, that sounds...stable.

TONG. Whatever. I don't know how long it'll last. He's clearly a rebound. And not just a rebound, an EX. It's like having sex with your hangover.

QUANG. I really didn't need that image.

TONG. And I really don't care.

(*She gives him a wink.*)

So...what did she look like?

QUANG. What did who look like?

TONG. The girl.

QUANG. She was okay.

TONG. Just okay?

QUANG. Yeah. She was actually kind of a dog. Like she fell off the ugly tree, hit every branch, and then landed on her face.

TONG. So she was smoking.

QUANG. Yeah.

TONG. And it was...good?

QUANG. It was okay.

TONG. Quang.

QUANG. I'm being real. It was fun for a minute, but I knew I was just throwing gas on a problem that needed water. I just wanted a second to forget about my shit, but I couldn't. I just kept thinking about you – about us – everything. I'm sorry. I really am. About everything.

TONG. I believe you.

(**QUANG** *and* **TONG** *lock eyes.*)

Do not look at me like that.

QUANG. Like what?

TONG. Like you're a hungry cartoon wolf and I'm an animated turkey leg.

QUANG. I'm not looking at you like nothing.

TONG. I've been with you for five years. Trust me, I know that look.

QUANG. It ain't my fault you look good tonight.

TONG. You stupid. I don't look good.

QUANG. I mean look at this t-shirt. No one fills out a T-shirt as well as you. I think I just dropped something. My JAW! And those jeans. Is that made outta beaver? 'Cause DAMN.

TONG. That doesn't even make sense.

QUANG. And there's that smile. The best smile I've ever witnessed. That smile that can make any bad day seem good.

TONG. Can you stop throwing lines at me?

QUANG. That last one's not a line.

> *(Their eyes lock.)*
>
> *(He leans over.)*
>
> *(They share a tender kiss.)*
>
> *(But she ultimately pushes him away.)*

TONG. No.

> **(QUANG** *sits back embarrassed.)*

QUANG. Cool, that wasn't embarrassing like at all.

TONG. I'm sorry.

QUANG. Don't be. I was overstepping.

TONG. Look, it's fun hanging out with you like this, but –

QUANG. I miss you.

TONG. Quang, don't.

QUANG. Do you not miss / me at all?

TONG. I need more than what you can give me right now.

QUANG. But don't you feel anything for me?

TONG. This has nothing to do with my feelings. This is about what I need. And what I need – right now – in my life...is more than just "You. Me. And a starry night sky to dream under."

QUANG. Do you not love me anymore?

TONG. Don't ask me that.

QUANG. Don't you?

[MUSIC NO. 07 – I DON'T GIVE A...]

(A beat drops.)

TONG. *(Rapped.)*
LOVE IS JUST SOME BULLSHIT STORY
GLORIOUS ON PAPER, BUT IN LIFE – A PURGATORY
BETWEEN HEARTACHES AND HEARTBREAKS, YOU
    FORSAKE YOUR OWN FATE
FOR SOME MOMENTARY MOMENT WHERE YOU'RE
    TRAPPED – INMATE
TAKE MY BALL OUT THIS POINTLESS GAME
OF FAIRY TALES THAT ALWAYS END IN PAIN
MY SONG IS NOW A SOLO, NO ROMANTIC REFRAINS
AN ORCHESTRA OF ONE, I'LL NEVER DU-ET AGAIN
DON'T COME AT ME WITH YOUR PITY OR YOUR SORROW
WE CAN HAVE FUN TODAY, I'LL DISAPPEAR TOMORROW
IF YOU'RE LOOKING FOR MORE,
YOU CHOSE THE WRONG DOOR
NOTHING LASTS FOREVER WHEN YOUR ASS IS POOR
DON'T TELL ME YOU WANNA BE WITH ME
FOR I GOT A LITTLE MAN WHOSE NEEDS I GOTTA MEET
MAKING SURE HE'S FED IS MY PRIORITY
EV'RYTHING ELSE – EMPTY LUXURIES

TONG.
SO DON'T ASK FOR MY HAND – THAT'S NOT WHO I AM
I'M A YELLA RHETT BUTLER – I DON'T GIVE NO DAMNS
I SURVIVED A CIVIL WAR – LOST ALL THAT I HAD
NOW I'M LOSING EVEN MORE IN THIS GODFORSAKEN
    LAND
SO IMMA KEEP RUNNING TILL I GET ME MINE
DON'T NEED NO RING, ROLLING SOLO'S FINE
THIS COUNTRY CAN HIT ME, IMMA GET RIGHT UP
NOTHING CAN STOP ME, I DON'T GIVE NO FUCKS
I'M JUST A SINGLE PLAYER – GOT NO TIME TO PLAY
I'M BUSTING MY ASS EV'RY NIGHT AND DAY
THIS IS WHO I AM IN THE U. S. OF A.
DON'T TELL ME YOU LOVE ME – GO THE FUCK AWAY.

(**QUANG** *walks away, dejected.*)

THAT GOES TO ANYONE WANNA GET WITH ME
ANY FINE FELLAS – YA WANNA GET WITH ME?
TAKE A CLOSE LOOK BEFORE YOU GET WITH ME
CUZ IF YOU'RE LOOKING FOR LOVE, DON'T WASTE YOUR
    TIME ON ME
I DON'T GIVE A SHIT, I DON'T GIVE A SHIT, GIVE A SHIT
I DON'T GIVE A SHIT, I DON'T GIVE A SHIT, GIVE A SHIT
I DON'T GIVE A SHIT, I DON'T GIVE A SHIT, GIVE A SHIT
I DON'T GIVE A...

(*The music ends.* **TONG** *is back in her trailer, alone.*)

Shit.

(*There's a knock at the door.*)

(**TONG** *takes a deep breath and answers it.*)

(*On the other side is* **BOBBY.**)

BOBBY. Greetings, pretty angel face love pumpkin.

TONG. Bobby, what are you doing here?

BOBBY. Tong have sad face.

TONG. I'm fine.

BOBBY. Bobby no like sad face.

TONG. Well, if we're gonna see each other, this is a face you're going to have to get used to.

BOBBY. That why Bobby is here. Bobby wanting to erase your face.

TONG. That sounds like a death threat.

BOBBY. *(Realizes what he said is incorrect.)* No. NO! Not erase face. Erase the part of face that is sad.

TONG. Thank you for the gesture, but there's a lot going on.

BOBBY. Like what?

TONG. Like…stuff you wouldn't understand.

BOBBY. Bobby would like to try.

> (**BOBBY** *takes a deep breath, musters up courage, does some stretches.)*

TONG. What are you doing?

BOBBY. Just…please sit down.

> (**TONG** *sits, confused.)*

TONG. Okay?

> (**BOBBY** *gets out a tape player and presses "PLAY.")*

[MUSIC NO. 08 – BOBBY'S PROPOSAL]

BOBBY. *(Sung.)*
THIS IS MAYBE CRAZY, BUT TONG IS PRETTY LADY
I YOUR FLUFFY BISCUIT, YOU MY SAUSAGE GRAVY

BOBBY.

I GOT BIG HEARTS FROM THE MOMENT I MET YOU
AND EV'RY DAY IN EV'RY WAY I NEED TO JUST GET YOU
OUR HEARTS MERGER
IN THIS LAND OF CHEESEBURGER

(Rapped.)

THERE'S NO PRECURSORS,
I WANT TO GO FURTHER

(Sung.)

YOU'RE THE GEORGE TO MY JEFFERSONS
RERUN TO MY WHAT'S HAPPENIN'
MORK TO MY MINDY
WKRP IN CINCINNATI
WILL YOU HAVE ME?
THIS RING MAY BE CRAPPY
AND MY WORDS KINDA SAPPY
PRINCESS AWESOME MAKE ME HAPPY
I DON'T STUTTER
FOR ME THERE IS NO ONE OTHER
YOU MAKE MY HEART FLUTTER
WANNA BE YOUR BREAD AND BUTTER
WHERE THE HECK ARE YOU GOING?
I DON'T KNOW BUT I'M KNOWING,
HOWEVER IMPOSSIBLE THIS IS –
I WANT TO BE YOUR NEW HUSBAND
WILL YOU MARRY ME – MARCIA BRADY...?
TONG. PLEASE MARRY ME.

8.

(Outside a dirty motel room, **QUANG** *drinks a beer while sitting on the stoop.)*

NHAN. *(Offstage.)* Quang!

*(***QUANG** *looks up and greets his approaching best friend.)*

QUANG. Hey man! Thanks for coming. Make yourself at home, I'll get you a drink –

NHAN. So this is where you've been staying?

QUANG. Well, it is where all my clothes currently reside so –

NHAN. Bro, this is place is –

QUANG. Complete dogshit. Yeah, I know.

NHAN. *(Trying to be positive.)* Yo, man, it's not that bad. It's still better than living in – like – a dumpster. Or under a bridge. Or... Mississippi.

QUANG. Did you bring what I asked?

NHAN. Yeah, man, all my stock is in the car. What do you want? A gold chain? A new watch? I picked up a couple of new-ish Betamax players last week –

QUANG. The sewing machine.

NHAN. You were serious about that?

QUANG. I sold my wedding ring and did a whole bunch of overtime these last couple of weeks. I got almost five hundred dollars here. I want a good one, not one of those plastic pieces of shit that'll break in a month.

NHAN. Why do you need a sewing machine? Is there a new sweatshop in town where you gotta provide your own gear?

QUANG. Tong used to make clothes for her brother when she was small. It made her feel needed, accomplished. It was some of her favorite memories. I think she might like making some stuff for Little Man. So do you have one?

NHAN. *(Disbelief.)* What are you doing, man?

QUANG. I'm trying to purchase some slightly used or perhaps illegally acquired goods from you.

NHAN. You're a captain of the South Vietnamese Air Force.

QUANG. God, shut up with that shit. That was me there. This is me here. And all "me here" wants is to give you five hundred dollars for a fucking sewing machine, so can I do that?

NHAN. You're a military man. You, out of all people, should know when you're fighting a losing battle.

QUANG. You think I don't know that? I know I already lost. I'm just trying to salvage what I got left.

NHAN. Look at me, bro. You know I care about you, right? I just wanna see you do well.

QUANG. So are you gonna hook me up?

NHAN. No.

QUANG. What do you mean no?

NHAN. It's time to let her go.

QUANG. Fuck off!

NHAN. That isn't going to help you OR her.

QUANG. You don't understand –

NHAN. I understand plenty. I've known you since you were eighteen years old – I've seen how you've struggled here these last five years. If you want to help her – if you want to help BOTH of you – give her more than a goddamn sewing machine. Go to the court house, grant Tong full custody of Little Man, and leave town.

QUANG. No fucking way.

NHAN. I'm your bro. And as your bro, I gotta be real with you – you two are no good for each other.

QUANG. That's not true.

NHAN. You don't know how to make each other happy anymore. She's with Bobby, you're in this shithole, and you're both broke. It's time to be proactive – give her what she needs and get the fuck out of here.

QUANG. But I love her.

NHAN. But she don't love you.

(*Beat.*)

She's not your girl anymore. It's time to accept that.

(**NHAN** *walks away as* **QUANG** *falls into a spotlight.*)

[MUSIC NO. 09 – I'LL FIX THIS]

(*Music drops.*)

QUANG. (*Sung.*)
YOU'RE NOT MY GIRL
I KNOW THAT NOW
I STILL LOVE YOU
SO THIS I VOW
I'LL DO WHAT'S RIGHT
I UNDERSTAND
I NEED TO FIX THIS EVEN THOUGH
I'M NOT YOUR MAN
IT MUST BE TOUGH
WHEN YOU'RE ALL ALONE
I KNOW I FAILED YOU

QUANG.

LET ME ATONE
OUR MARRIAGE ENDS
BUT YOU'RE STILL MY HOME
IN MY SOUL I KNOW I OWE YA
EVEN THOUGH YOU'RE GONE
IT'S CRAZY
WE BROKE APART
I BLAME ME
I BROKE YOUR HEART
IT'S ON ME
THOUGH YA WANT AN END
I GOTTA FIND A WAY TO MAKE YOU SMILE AGAIN
PLEASE SAVE ME
I FUCKED THIS UP
I HATE ME
I LOST YOUR LOVE
IT'S ON ME
THOUGHYOU WANT AN END
I GOTTA FIND A WAY TO MAKE YOU WHOLE AGAIN

(Rapped.)

I GOT YOU, BABY, THO I'M NOT YOUR MAN, I GOT A PLAN
THO THIS DANCE HAS TO END,
IT'S NOT MY END, I'LL TRANSCEND
GONNA GIVE YOU ALL OF ME
TO REMEDY THIS TRAGEDY
GONNA GIVE YA WHAT YOU NEED
TO GET YOU BACK ON YOUR FEET
EVEN IF IT'S MUCH TOO LATE,
I'LL CREATE A BRAND NEW FATE
I CAN FIN'LY ILLUSTRATE
HOW TO BE YOUR PERFECT MATE

(Sung.)

NO MORE TEARS,

NO MORE FEAR,

I AM HERE, BABY
NO MORE LIES,
I WILL RISE,
I KNOW IT'S DO OR DIE
I SWEAR TO SET THINGS RIGHT
I CAN SEE
WHAT YOU NEED
TO BE FREE, BABY
I WILL SHOW YOU
HOW MUCH I LOVE YOU

9.

*(**HUONG** joins **TONG**, folding laundry.)*

HUONG. You look tired.

TONG. *(Not great.)* I'm great!

HUONG. The new job is good?

TONG. I push a button, it cuts paper, all day long, a hundred miles away from here. It's a dream come true.

HUONG. How's Bobby?

TONG. We broke up.

HUONG. You did?

TONG. He wanted something I couldn't give him.

HUONG. And what's that?

TONG. Mom, he sang at my face. It freaked me out.

HUONG. Are you sure you want to be alone right now?

TONG. I'm not alone. I have you, I have Little Man. A veritable cornucopia of endless responsibility. So fulfilling.

*(**HUONG** watches **TONG** as she robotically folds clothes.)*

HUONG. I have to tell you something.

TONG. What's that? You have another young Vietnamese beautician you want to pimp to me?

HUONG. Listen to me. I look at you. I see you. You work so hard. He never could provide. I thought – you needed to be saved.

TONG. What are you talking about?

HUONG. I just wanted you to have a better life.

TONG. You're sounding crazy.

HUONG. I ruined your marriage.

TONG. *(Consoles her mom.)* Mom, you're a pain in my ass, but you did not ruin my marriage.

HUONG. *(Confesses.)* I'm the one who contacted Quang's wife. I'm the one who told her he was here.

TONG. What?

HUONG. Quang's broke. He never could provide. I was trying to look out for you.

TONG. You did *what*?

HUONG. I wanted to give you the chance to find someone better –

TONG. I wasn't looking for anyone better.

HUONG. I didn't know –

TONG. MOM! This is my life. You fucked up my marriage.

HUONG. I know.

TONG. I'm drowning. I don't need you to add weights to my legs as well.

HUONG. You're not drowning.

TONG. I'm not? I'm a single mom with a shit-ass job and a kid who can't learn the fucking language in a country that looks right through us.

HUONG. I know I messed up. I'm sorry.

TONG. You did more than mess up. You made my life harder and it was already really fucking hard.

HUONG. Don't say that.

TONG. I can't even look at you right now.

HUONG. Tong.

TONG. I just... I need to go.

HUONG. Where are you going to go?

TONG. Don't worry, Mom. I'm not going to leave you. But you messed up really bad this time. I just... I need to go for a walk. Can you please bring Little Man to school? And not mess that up too?

> *(Lights down on a distraught **HUONG** as we follow **TONG** out the door.)*
>
> *(She looks around, not knowing where she should go.)*
>
> *(She finally picks a direction and walks...)*

10.

*(**HUONG** walks **LITTLE MAN** to school.)*

LITTLE MAN. Bà Ngoai, why no voice to Little Man today?

*(**HUONG** looks at **LITTLE MAN**, gives him a smile, and continues on.)*

Little Man wants to hear one of *Bà Ngoai*'s bio-pic stories about Rambo Land. Can *Bà Ngoai* voice Little Man a Rambo Land story?

*(**HUONG** shakes her head and continues on.)*

Bà Ngoai! Voice to Little Man! Voice! Please?

*(**HUONG** grits her teeth, but shakes her head.)*

Grandma!

*(**HUONG** can't take it anymore.)*

HUONG. Shhhh. Your mom and your teacher think it's better you don't hear Vietnamese anymore. Which means I have to watch what I can say to you since that's the only language I know.

LITTLE MAN. You don't know Cheeseburger?

HUONG. Nope.

LITTLE MAN. I can teach you.

HUONG. I'm an old dog. I'm not like your mommy. Grandma's never been good at learning stuff. Never needed it. I knew how to get what I needed without books.

LITTLE MAN. In Rambo Land?

HUONG. Yes, in Vietnam.

LITTLE MAN. Because you're Vietnamese.

HUONG. That's correct.

LITTLE MAN. And I'm a Cheeseburger.

HUONG. NO.

> *(***HUONG*** lifts ***LITTLE MAN*** and sits him down next to her on a park bench.)*

You are not a Cheeseburger. You may be a citizen of Cheeseburger land, you may speak in Cheeseburger, but your heart is Vietnamese. Like mine. Do you understand?

LITTLE MAN. Then why does everyone want me to stop talking in Vietnamese?

HUONG. Because you live here and apparently Cheeseburgers have no room on their plate for anything besides meat and potatoes.

LITTLE MAN. How far away is Vietnam?

HUONG. It's...not far.

LITTLE MAN. It's not?

HUONG. No. It's actually...just right outside this town.

LITTLE MAN. It is?

HUONG. Yep. Just past the city limits, that's where people that talk and look just like you and me live.

LITTLE MAN. How big is it?

HUONG. Enormous. Bigger than this town. Bigger than the whole country of America. That's why people here in Arkansas can be a bit mean to us sometimes. 'Cause they're jealous that there's so little of them and so many of us.

LITTLE MAN. That's why they're mean?

HUONG. Yep. And I'm going to tell you something that they won't. They do it because those people want to be just like you. Because you're special.

LITTLE MAN. I'm special?

HUONG. You are. Because when you're in a small shit-town like this one, where everyone and everything is the same, being different means you have the chance to become magical.

LITTLE MAN. I do?

HUONG. That's why we left Vietnam, because there you would have never been able to find your magic. Here however, you will. But getting magic is hard. It's real hard. Because all these people here will be testing you. They'll be pushing you to make you feel small. That's so you'll never learn how powerful you can become. And I promise you, little man, you are powerful. But it's not going to be easy. Especially here.

But if you keep them from ever hurting your heart, you will be able to shape worlds with your magic.

LITTLE MAN. I will?

HUONG. You will. I promise you, you will.

And if you ever get too sad because of their taunts, just remember there's more Vietnam in this world than America.

LITTLE MAN. Is that true, Grandma?

HUONG. Well, it's a story. And stories are all that matter in this world because it's the only things we get to keep in our hearts.

LITTLE MAN. I love your stories, *Bà Ngoai*.

HUONG. And I love telling them. But this may be my last story for a little bit, okay? Because this next test is for you to learn how to speak and think just like them. For that is where your magic will come from, Little Man… by using their words. And Grandma doesn't want to hold you back any longer.

LITTLE MAN. Okay.

(She hugs him.)

HUONG. I love you, Little Man.

LITTLE MAN. I love you too, Bà Ngoai.

HUONG. But you learn that shit quick, because Grandma has way more stories to tell.

(She signals for him to jump into her arms for them to exit.)

(Exit language:)

Whoa, you're getting heavy. What have you been eating? Rocks?

(As they exit.) Come on, let's go get Grandma a beer.

11.

(Outside Quang's motel room.)

*(***TONG*** *approaches, takes a deep breath, knocks on the door – and immediately runs away.)*

QUANG. Tong?

TONG. Quang! What are you doing here?!

QUANG. You knocked on my door.

TONG. Are you sure?

QUANG. Is everything okay?

TONG. I have something I need to tell you.

QUANG. What is it?

TONG. It was my mom who contacted your wife. She was the one who did that to you.

QUANG. Yeah, I sorta put that together already.

TONG. You did? I'm so sorry. She had no business doing that. I just...maybe if that hadn't happened, maybe –

QUANG. I fucked up too. Big time. That's on me. And then what happened in Houston.

TONG. We don't need to rehash. We're cool.

(They awkwardly stand there for a minute. It's clear they want more, but don't know how to get there.)

I should go –

QUANG. Actually, I'm glad you're here. I have something I need to – just don't go anywhere.

TONG. Where are you –

(**QUANG** *ducks into his apartment.*)

TONG. Quang? Hello? Quang?

(*He returns holding an official-looking envelope.*)

QUANG. Here you go.

TONG. What is this?

QUANG. Official documents that change our status forever. I know you're not my girl. I just wanted to show that I know that now.

TONG. Are these divorce papers?

QUANG. I want you to know that I can do this. For you. For Little Man.

(**TONG** *looks at the envelope.*)

TONG. Really? So you just went out and did it?

QUANG. I was being proactive. You needed that from me, right? There it is.

(**TONG** *keeps looking at the envelope, but doesn't take it.*)

Tong?

TONG. Sorry. This is all more – wow – I didn't expect – God, what is happening to my eyes?

QUANG. So do you not want this?

(*He extends the envelope to her.*)

TONG. No, I'll take it.

(*She finally takes it and stares at it for a moment. She puts it in her pocket.*)

I guess that's that then. You're like super not-my-husband anymore.

(She reaches out, shakes his hand.)

Great, so...see you around, Quang.

(She turns to leave, but his hand won't let go.)

QUANG. Wait.

TONG. Yes, what is it? What's happening?

QUANG. You're, um, not going to open it?

TONG. You told me what was inside.

QUANG. No, I didn't.

TONG. You said they were divorce papers.

QUANG. No, I didn't actually say they were divorce papers. I may have led you to believe they were divorce papers, but I never actually said outright it was divorce papers.

TONG. Is this not divorce papers?

QUANG. I don't know.

TONG. What is it?

QUANG. Just open it!

TONG. I'm not doing shit if you're going to yell at me.

QUANG. Will you open it? Please? I want it to be a surprise.

*(**TONG** opens it.)*

TONG. Cool. It's divorce papers. Thanks.

QUANG. It's not divorce papers – you really should work on reading English as well as speaking it.

TONG. It's legal forms. How am I supposed to know what it is?

QUANG. Read the address.

TONG. 700 East Main.

Wait, is this... Quang, is this the deed to Paul's Dairy Diner?

QUANG. It's a rental agreement to your new EAST MAIN Dairy Diner.

TONG. Why?

QUANG. Because you deserve to be happy. And I just wanted to show you I still know how to do that.

TONG. *(Moved.)* You got me the diner.

QUANG. You're right. You don't need a man, you need a partner. I'm sorry I wasn't one before.

(**QUANG** *gets down on one knee.*)

TONG. What is happening???

QUANG. I did this all wrong the first time. I wanna do it right this time, okay? Tong Thi Tran...will you let me work for you?

(*He pulls out the diner keys, offers them to her like an engagement ring.*)

Tong?

TONG. God, you're so stupid. Stand up.

QUANG. Is that a no?

[MUSIC NO. 10 – PROPOSAL (REPRISE)]

TONG. *(Rapped.)*
YOUR TIMING IS SHIT, BUT I GOTTA ADMIT
YOUR STUPID-ASS FACE IS HARD TO RESIST
YOU STILL MAKE ME SMILE, I STILL LIKE YOUR GAME
BUT GETTING BACK WITH YOU, I'D HAVE TO BE INSANE

QUANG.
SO WILL YOU MARRY ME?

TONG.
YA FUCKED IN THE HEAD

QUANG.

ONLY FOR YOU, BABY
ARE WE GONNA STAY WED?

TONG.

THIS ALL STARTED MESSY,
IT MAY STILL BE A MESS

QUANG.

I WANT YOU FOREVER –

TONG.

MY ANSWER IS YES!

QUANG.

HOLD UP BABY
CAN'T BELIEVE YOU JUST SAID IT.

TONG.

YOU'RE THE ONE FOR ME
THIS LOVE IS AUTHENTIC

QUANG.

TOGETHER FOREVER,
THIS SHIT'LL BE EPIC

TONG.

WE'RE GONNA STAY MARRIED,
CAN'T BELIEVE I JUST SAID IT

QUANG.

WHERE THE HELL ARE WE GOING?

TONG.

WE DON'T KNOW BUT WE KNOWING

QUANG.

HOWEVER IMPOSSIBLE THIS IS

TONG.

WE'LL MAKE THIS PLACE OUR NEW HOMELAND

TONG & QUANG.
HOME
WE'LL MAKE IT OUR HOME
WHERE THE HELL ARE WE GOING?
WE DON'T KNOW BUT WE KNOWING
HOWEVER IMPOSSIBLE THIS IS
WE'LL MAKE THIS PLACE OUR NEW HOMELAND
HOME
WE'LL MAKE IT HOME

> *(They kiss. The kinda kiss Molly Ringwald always dreams of getting in all those 80s movies.)*
>
> *(They dance…)*
>
> *(As they do, the projection of years click forward from 1980 to 2015.)*
>
> *(**PLAYWRIGHT** enters with glasses and sweaters for **TONG** and **QUANG**, they put them on, transforming themselves from thirty-five to seventy.)*
>
> *(Onstage, the world transitions back to…)*

EPILOGUE

*(2015. **TONG** walks over, puts on glasses, and pushes the Playwright's laptop closed.)*

TONG. I change mind. Don't write any of that down. This is not good story to tell. Grandchildren do not want to hear story about grandma and grandpa sex life. That is very inappropriate.

PLAYWRIGHT. We can edit that part out.

TONG. Edit it all out. Write something different. You not even telling it correctly anyway. I don't know kung fu. You think I know kung fu? No, I just slap people. I very good at slapping.

PLAYWRIGHT. Oh, I know.

TONG. This story will not make grandchildren feel proud.

PLAYWRIGHT. Sure it will.

TONG. You live it as well. When you little, it not make you feel proud. Or do you not remember yelling at Mommy and Daddy, "Why you name me Qui? Why you give me Vietnamese name no one say right? Why you not name me something American like a Bathalalala –

PLAYWRIGHT. Bartholomew.

TONG. Batalalew.

PLAYWRIGHT. Bartholomew.

TONG. Butt Tut A Two.

PLAYWRIGHT. You nailed it.

TONG. The point is...you were not proud.

PLAYWRIGHT. I was a stupid kid.

TONG. No. You were just a kid who wanted to feel like normal kid. We wanted to give you that.

PLAYWRIGHT. And you did.

I'm here, aren't I?

TONG. This is what I want to say – we did not tell you our story so you would have to tell those stories later. We tell you our story so you can learn how to tell your own. So you can learn to be proud in yourself.

PLAYWRIGHT. And that's the thing, Mom. I am proud. And it's BECAUSE of those stories. That's exactly why I'm writing this. Do you not get it?

[MUSIC NO. 11 – POOR YELLA REDNECKS (FINALE)]

(Rapped.)

I WRIT THIS – SO MY KIDS COULD WITNESS
A TALE WHERE THE YELLA KIDS GET TO BE THE
  PROTAGONISTS
INSTEAD OF SOME WHITE GUY STEALING THE SPOTLIGHT
WHICH MAKES MY LITTLE GUYS FEEL LESS THAN THOSE
  OTHER GUYS
I DON'T WANNA TELL THEM
HOLLYWOOD'S FAILED THEM
WHEN I FLIP ON A SCREEN –
I WANNA SEE THEM
SO I PUT MY PEN TO THE PAGE,
WITH MY EYES TO ONE AIM
TAKE THE YELLA STARS FROM THE SKY
TO LIGHT UP A STAGE

(He steps into a spotlight...)

SO STEP BACK SUCKER,
IMMA FIGHT TILL THEY GET IT
ANYTHING LESS THAN EXCELLENCE,
YOU CAN FUCKING FORGET IT
ME AND MY PEEPS COMIN' ATCHA,
YOU CAN READ IT ON REDDIT

THESE STORIES AIN'T ALLEGORIES,
MY PEOPLE ACTU'LY BLED IT
FUCK ANYONE TRY TO MAKE YOU TALK DIFF'RENT
THEY LISTENED, NOW IT'S HARD FOR ME
TO TALK TO MY OWN PARENTS
THEY SAID ASSIMILATION HAS SOME GOOD MERITS
BUT THE COST IS QUITE A LOT JUST TO SOUND GENERIC
SO I'M TELLING THEIR STORY,
CELEBRATING THEIR STORY
SPITTING LYRICS RHYTHMIC'LY TO ELUCIDATE THEIR
 STORY
FOR THEY DESERVE GLORY,
THESE PEEPS THAT CAME BEFORE ME
FOR BUSTING THEIR ASSES, MAKING A HOME HERE FOR ME

(Spotlight on **NHAN** *at the club…)*

NHAN. *(Rapped.)*

SO THROW ON YOUR SMOOTH SHIT, YOU WANNA DO THIS
WE KICKING A.Z.N'S LIKE A SHAW BROTHERS MOVIE
STAND UP, HOMIES, SHOW US YOUR PRIDE
FUCK ALL THE HATERS, THIS MOMENT IS OUR TIME
 (POOR YELLA)

*(***QUANG*** and* **TONG** *at the pickup…)*

QUANG.

WE'RE GONNA THRIVE IN THIS FOREIGN LAND
BUT TODAY WE'RE GONNA DO WHATEVER WE CAN
TO CREATE A PLACE WHERE WE ALL CAN STAND
DEFYING ALL THE HATERS WHO SAY WE CAN'T

TONG.

I'M CLIMBING THESE LADDERS,
ADAPTING THROUGH DISASTERS
NO MONEY IN MY POCKET BUT I'M RICH WHERE IT
 MATTERS
WON'T STOP TILL WE'VE WON, SON
SWINGING FOR THAT HOME RUN

TONG.
LIKE THE SONG SAYS, "IMMIGRANTS –

COMPANY.
WE GET THE JOB DONE!"

(**HUONG** *and* **LITTLE MAN** *at home...*)

HUONG.
EVEN IF THEY MAD AT YOU, YOU GOTTA BE TRUE TO YOU
EV'RY SCAR YOU WEAR, YOU SHOW THE SHIT THAT YOU
WENT THROUGH
YA GOTTA STAND STRONG, BE STRONG, HEADSTRONG, YA
AIN'T WRONG
SO COME ON LISTEN CLOSE, THIS HERE'S OUR FIGHT
SONG

PLAYWRIGHT. *(Rapped.)*
POOR YELLA REDNECKS
WE DEMAND RESPECT
AIN'T GOT ALOTTA MONEY
BUT WE'RE STILL GOD-DAMN PERFECT
HAVE PRIDE IN US, SON
LISTEN TO OUR REASON
WE'RE CLIMBING MOUNTAINS WHILE THE REST OF THEM
ARE SLEEPING

(Commands.) Sing!

COMPANY. *(Sung.)*
POOR YELLA REDNECKS
WE DEMAND RESPECT
AIN'T GOT ALOTTA MONEY
BUT WE'RE STILL GOD-DAMN PERFECT
RISE UP, SON
LISTEN TO OUR REASON
WE'RE CLIMBING MOUNTAINS WHILE THE REST OF THEM
ARE SLEEPING

POOR YELLA REDNECKS

WE DEMAND RESPECT

AIN'T GOT ALOTTA MONEY

BUT WE'RE STILL DAMN PERFECT

RISE UP, SON

LISTEN TO OUR REASON

WE'RE CLIMBING MOUNTAINS WHILE THE REST OF THEM
ARE SLEEPING

COMPANY (EXCEPT PLAYWRIGHT & TONG).

(Sung.)

POOR YELLA REDNECKS

WE DEMAND RESPECT

AIN'T GOT ALOTTA MONEY

BUT WE'RE STILL
GOD-DAMN PERFECT

RISE UP, SON

LISTEN TO OUR REASON

WE'RE CLIMBING
MOUNTAINS

WHILE THE REST OF
THEM ARE SLEEPING

TONG.

(Rapped.)

DON'T GOT A LOT OF
OPTIONS,

DON'T GOT A LOT OF CASH

WE GOT A LOT OF
PROBLEMS,

TONG & PLAYWRIGHT.

YOU CAN KISS OUR ASS!

TONG.

WE POOR AS FUCK

YELLA AS WELL

NOTHING STOPPING US
CUZ

TONG & PLAYWRIGHT.

WE MAD AS HELL!

COMPANY. *(Sung.)*

POOR YELLA REDNECKS

WE DEMAND RESPECT

AIN'T GOT ALOTTA MONEY

BUT WE'RE STILL DAMN PERFECT

RISE UP, SON

LISTEN TO OUR REASON

WE'RE CLIMBING MOUNTAINS WHILE THE REST OF THEM
ARE SLEEPING

(Lights down.)

www.ingramcontent.com/pod-product-compliance
Lightning Source LLC
Chambersburg PA
CBHW070331120726
47909CB00008B/2676